The critics roared!

"Hilarious, rib-tickling fantasy, funniest on record!"
—Hartford Courant

"Mad yarn, cockeyed humor, needle-sharp, ironic jabs!"
—San Francisco Chronicle

"The Psychiatric Quarterly" roared!
They're mad about this book. They called it an "astonishing combination of amazingly good-humored satire, science-fiction, fantasy and practicality . . ."

THE MOUSE THAT ROARED!
is a completely off-beat, hilarious book that got famous because it got everyone right in the funnybone!

THE MOUSE THAT ROARED
BY LEONARD WIBBERLEY

BANTAM PATHFINDER EDITIONS
TORONTO / NEW YORK / LONDON

A NATIONAL GENERAL COMPANY

*This low-priced Bantam Book
has been completely reset in a type face
designed for easy reading, and was printed
from new plates. It contains the complete
text of the original hard-cover edition.*
NOT ONE WORD HAS BEEN OMITTED.

RLI: VLM 8 (VLR 8–9)
—————————————
IL 9–adult

THE MOUSE THAT ROARED

*A Bantam Book / published by arrangement with
Little, Brown and Company*

PRINTING HISTORY

Serialized in THE SATURDAY EVENING POST *December 1954—
January 1955 as The Day New York Was Invaded
Little, Brown edition published February 1955
12 printings through October 1963*

Bantam edition published June 1959

2nd printing .... July 1959	6th printing .... April 1962
3rd printing ..... October 1959	7th printing .... April 1962
4th printing ... September 1960	8th printing .... July 1962
5th printing .... April 1962	9th printing ... December 1962

Bantam Pathfinder edition published September 1964

11th printing .. November 1964	16th printing .... May 1967
12th printing ...... April 1965	17th printing .... July 1967
13th printing .. September 1966	18th printing .... October 1968
14th printing .. December 1966	19th printing .... August 1969
15th printing ... February 1967	20th printing ..... August 1969

21st printing ..... January 1970
New Bantam edition published January 1971
2nd printing .... May 1971   3rd printing ... December 1971
Bantam Pathfinder edition published November 1972

4th printing
5th printing

All rights reserved.
Copyright © 1954, 1955 by the Curtis Publishing Company.
Copyright © 1955 by Leonard Wibberley.
*This book may not be reproduced in whole or in part, by
mimeograph or any other means, without permission.
For information address: Little, Brown and Company,
34 Beacon Street, Boston, Massachusetts 02106.*

Published simultaneously in the United States and Canada

———————————————————————————————

*Bantam Books are published by Bantam Books, Inc., a National
General company. Its trade-mark, consisting of the words "Bantam
Books" and the portrayal of a bantam, is registered in the United
States Patent Office and in other countries. Marca Registrada.
Bantam Books, Inc., 666 Fifth Avenue, New York, N.Y. 10019.*

———————————————————————————————

PRINTED IN THE UNITED STATES OF AMERICA

To all the little nations who over the centuries have done what they could to attain and preserve their freedom. It is from one of them that I am sprung.

LEONARD WIBBERLEY

THE MOUSE
THAT ROARED

1

THE DUCHY OF GRAND FENWICK LIES IN A PRECIPITOUS FOLD of the northern Alps and embraces in its tumbling landscape portions of three valleys, a river, one complete mountain with an elevation of two thousand feet and a castle. There are, in the northern part of the duchy, where the slopes of the surrounding peaks provide both the right soil and exposure, four hundred acres of vineyards. These produce a small black grape of a particularly pleasant bouquet from which is obtained the Pinot Grand Fenwick, of which the possession of a small stock is the crowning achievement of any connoisseur of wines.

In six centuries the output of Pinot Grand Fenwick has never exceeded two thousand bottles a year. In bad years it has fallen off to as little as five hundred bottles, and there are still some alive who recall the disastrous year of 1913 when, due to late snows and unseasonable rains, no more than three hundred and fifty bottles were produced. That year has remained more sharply etched in the memories of the lovers of wine than the subsequent twelve months when the news of the outbreak of the Great War was softened for them by the knowledge that the vineyards of Grand Fenwick had produced a bumper crop of the small black grapes.

The duchy is no more than five miles long and three wide. Its sovereign lord has been for nearly six centuries either a duke or a duchess, and its national language, surprisingly, English. But to explain how all this came about, it is necessary to go back to the founding of the duchy in 1370 by the first duke, Roger Fenwick.

Roger Fenwick, of whom an indifferent but interesting portrait is to be found in the council chamber of the castle which dominates the duchy from the top of the two-thousand-foot mountain, had the misfortune to be

born the seventh son of an English knight. Of his brothers
only two survived their fifth year, but even so his father's
meager resources had long run out when the time came
for Roger to be sent into the world. It was decided,
therefore, that the boy should go to Oxford University
where he might, by earnest application to his books, secure employment either in the church, as a chronicler, or
in the train of some gentleman of means. But before he
was fourteen, Roger left Oxford; not that he could not
endure education, but that he was likely to have starved
to death before his tutoring was complete.

In the few fragments that remain of his own story, he
records that he learned but three things in two years at
Oxford. The first, on which he placed the greatest value,
was that "Yea" might be turned into "Nay" and vice versa
if a sufficient quantity of wordage was applied to the
matter. The second was that in any argument, the victor
is always right, and the third that though the pen is
mightier than the sword, the sword speaks louder and
stronger at any given moment.

After leaving Oxford, Roger did not return to the home
of his father, nor seek aid from his two surviving brothers.
Instead, being accomplished in the use of the long bow,
he joined the army of Edward III as a bowman at five
shillings a day plus plunder, was promoted to mounted
bowman, then man at arms, and finally, after the victory
at Poitiers, knight.

At that time he was twenty-four and chose to remain
in France with the garrison of the Black Prince. That he
did so was not so much a matter of patriotism as of prac-
ticing his profession of arms. He followed the Black
Prince into Spain in the campaign which briefly put
Pedro the Cruel back on his throne of Castile, and then,
leaving the English Army, formed a free company of
his own.

The company was not a large one. It consisted of himself, his squire and forty bowmen. But what it lacked in
numbers it made up in practical experience in warfare,
and Sir Roger Fenwick was able to hire himself to Charles
the Wise of France in his war with the Navarrese. Sir

Roger had, and he was at no great pains to disguise the matter, no more loyalty to France than he had to England. Indeed, it is recorded that on the eve of one battle between a French host on one side and a mixed army of English and Navarrese on the other, he decided to fight with the French only on the promise of their commander, Bertrand du Guesclin, that he would supply him with a new suit of armor in addition to his regular hire.

At the conclusion of the campaign Sir Roger had risen to such esteem as a fighting man that he was commissioned by Charles to take a company of men of his own raising and capture, for the king, a castle in the southern reaches of France, bordering the Alps, whose owner had sided consistently with the king's enemies. Had Charles been less concerned with other matters, he might have gained some inkling of what was going to happen from the men Sir Roger picked for the expedition.

He chose none but Englishmen, a robust, thieving, fighting horde whose lives were forfeit if they ever returned to their own country for crimes ranging from cutting purses to cutting throats. With these Sir Roger had no difficulty whatever in storming and taking the castle. And when this was done, far from turning the fortress over to Charles, he raised his own flag on the main keep, summoned the tenants from the adjacent lands and announced that he was their new duke and that they were from henceforth, liege men of the duchy of Grand Fenwick.

Some objected, demanding to see the patents of his nobility; whereupon Sir Roger flung his broadsword on the table before him and announced that that was patent enough.

"I have seen no king seated upon a throne by Almighty God," he said, "but many who mounted there over a pile of broken heads. What is good enough for kings is good enough for dukes." That was the end of the matter. He claimed the territory around for as many as ten arrow flights to the north and south of the castle and six to the east and west and so the duchy of Grand Fenwick came to be established.

Its early years were, it is true, tumultuous. Charles twice sent expeditions against Sir Roger and they were twice repulsed through the inability of the French to learn anything of the power of the English longbow. Successive sovereigns made successive attempts but with no more result. And in the end, with the passing of the years, the Fenwick claim became so strong, and the royal claim so remote, that the duchy was officially recognized as an independent and sovereign state and its national flag, a double-headed eagle saying "Yea" from one beak and "Nay" from another, accepted by the nations of the world.

The centuries rolled by without any expansion or contraction of the territory. By remarkable good fortune, Sir Roger had chosen to establish his duchy in a spot which lay on no great trade route, possessed no mines of precious metals or metals of any kind, had no harbors or great waterways and, indeed, nothing whatever to commend it to a conqueror. The portions of the three valleys which lay within its borders were reasonably but not overwhelmingly fertile. They produced enough food for its inhabitants and nothing but wine to export. The hillsides, where the ground was poorer, yet supported sufficient grass to graze flocks of sheep which provided meat and wool, and the duchy was, until the turn of the twentieth century, unsought, unknown, self-supporting and free.

It might well have remained in that happy state had it not been for the natural increase in its population and the equally natural decrease in the fertility of its soil. At the turn of the twentieth century the population was four thousand. By the commencement of World War I, it was four thousand five hundred. By World War II due to no small extent to the reduction in infant mortality, it had risen to six thousand. The need arose to import food and clothing, and for the first time in six hundred years Grand Fenwick, which had lustily maintained its independence from the outside world, was compelled to look around for some method of increasing its exports to earn the additional money essential to its expanding needs.

A proposal to augment the revenue obtained from the sale of the esteemed Pinot Grand Fenwick by watering the wine divided the duchy sharply into two bitterly opposed camps. One camp, the Dilutionists, insisted that the addition of as little as ten per cent water to the fermentation vats would make the duchy self-supporting again. The change in the quality of the product, they insisted, would not be noticed since eighty per cent of the vintage was bought by Americans who drank by label rather than by content.

"Wine into Water" became their slogan in the election year of 1956, it was supported by earnest statements of doctors and wine masters who asserted that the only beverage healthier than pure wine was wine mixed with water, which they pointed out, could be drunk without harm by little children.

The opposing party, the Anti-Dilutionists condemned the whole proposal as sacrilege. To water currency, as had become the practice in all the great nations of the world by the issuing of printing-press money, they maintained, was to cheat a man of his wealth. But to water wine was to cheat him of that for which he accumulated wealth. It was to discourage the struggle of every man towards a better standard of living by reducing the standard to the point where it was no longer worth struggling for.

"Those who would add water to Pinot Grand Fenwick," thundered the Count of Mountjoy, silver-haired leader of the Anti-Dilutionists, "would cheapen every work of art in the world so that there would be no such thing as a masterpiece but only a hundred million imitations of what was once a unique work. They would put the Mona Lisa on a postage stamp, and use the sublime words of our immortal bard Roger Bentshield to sell cigarettes. The wine is the blood of our grapes. It cannot and must not be diluted. This monstrous proposal," he continued, "is the result of the influence of foreign ideologies. It is traceable to the cant of the Communists in their cramped

Kremlin caves, on the one hand, and the wiles of the capitalists in their scintillating American skyscrapers, on the other. The freedom, the honor, the future, and the intrinsic worth of Grand Fenwick depends on a resounding 'NO' to this monstrous plot at the polls next March."

The polls did resound in March, when all ten delegates to the Council of Freedom, the parliament of Grand Fenwick, were to be elected. But when the ballots had been counted it was found that Dilutionists and Anti-Dilutionists were tied with five delegates each. In more prosperous days, the parliament would have tendered its resignation and another election been held, for it was the belief of the duchy that no nation can be governed well unless there is a majority which can impose its will upon a minority. A complete balance of pros and antis could produce nothing but deadlock.

However, with spring planting in progress, with every hand needed to till and to sow or tend to the lambing, the duchy could not afford a second election. And so the matter was referred to the sovereign lady, the Duchess Gloriana XII, a pretty girl of twenty-two, and a direct descendant of the doughty Sir Roger who had founded the state.

The meeting at which the crisis was laid before the duchess was a historic one, which, though ignored by the outside world, nonetheless warranted a two-column head-line on the front page of the *Fenwick Freeman*, the only newspaper published in the tiny nation. The delegates, clad in their medieval costumes, filed into the council chamber of the castle in which the parliament assembled, escorted by the sergeant at arms, carrying the mace.

The sergeant at arms laid the mace upon the ancient Table of State behind which the duchess was seated, her-self clad in the high-bodiced gown of the Middle Ages and wearing a ducal coronet prettily upon her head. The delegates then bowed solemnly to her and respectfully seated themselves to hear her opening address.

They were all of them middle-aged men, quite old enough to be her father. Each could recall her as a tiny girl who had at one time or another taken a ride in their carts (for they were all, except the Count of Mountjoy, farmers), coaxed pears or grapes from them, gone to school with their children and later taken part in the annual longbow contests. Then, but a year ago, her father the duke had died, leaving her to take over as ruler, and with that appalling suddenness which is the cross of nobility, she had had to change from neighbor to leader, from young girl to ruling lady, from fellow human to the symbol and strength of the nation.

This was the first parliament Gloriana had been called upon to open and despite the composure of her bearing she was somewhat nervous about it. She had spent much of the night before preparing her address from the throne, careful to skirt the political issues which had so recently reft the country, and dealing only with those topics which were noncontroversial.

Unfortunately, the only noncontroversial topic she could find was the weather, and even that, she discovered, was not completely neutral ground. For the kind of weather that would suit the winegrowers of the north, would not suit the wheat and barley raisers of the south. And so she limited herself to hoping that the duchy would be blessed with weather acceptable to all and that by continuing with that industry and self-reliance which had in the past been characteristic of the nation, Grand Fenwick would pull through the difficult times which lay ahead to continued peace and prosperity.

Her address was greeted with a robust round of applause, for all the delegates present looked upon their duchess as part daughter, and part ruler for whom they would willingly lay down their lives at any moment. There were cries of "Long live Duchess Gloriana the Twelfth" and then the time came for the majority leader to reply to the throne.

Since the crux of the crisis lay in the fact that there was no majority leader, it had been agreed at a bipartisan caucus that the leaders of the two parties should each make an address, presenting his side of the question for decision by the duchess.

The Count of Mountjoy, looking quite splendid in his

multicolored trunk hose, jerkin, and cape with flowing
sleeves, made the first speech. With the election over, he
was now prepared to be less fanatical on the subject of
Anti-Dilutionism and put the matter crisply, saying that
while the watering of Grand Pinot might in the first instance produce some gain, in the end it must result in the
discrediting of the wine and the total loss of all revenues
from its export.

Mr. David Benter, a dogged, stocky man, slow of
speech and thought, who lead the Dilutionists, then put
his side of the case.

It was not proposed to add more than ten per cent of
water by volume to the wine, he stated. This would certainly not destroy its bouquet, but, on the other hand, it
would greatly increase the output and the additional revenue if budgeted with practicality, and would ensure that
the duchy would be able to import the goods and food-
stuffs needed. What plans had the Anti-Dilutionists to offer which would achieve the same results?

Mountjoy did not reply directly to that question, pre-
ferring to return to his attack on the Dilutionist program.
Even if it might be held—and certainly no gentleman
could countenance such a belief—that the addition of ten
per cent of water to the famous Pinot would not harm
its bouquet and its reputation, what guarantee was there
that the amount added would be restricted to ten per
cent as the Dilutionists were now maintaining?

A ten per cent increase in revenue from wine exports
might be sufficient for present needs. But there was no
surety that those needs would not increase. Prices of food
and wool were rising on the world market. More revenue
would be needed next year; probably more still the year
after. Did the Dilutionists believe that they could just
continue adding more and more water until the famous
Pinot was no better than some of the cheap wines produced by France, consumed by Frenchmen, and undoubtedly responsible for the loss of national pride and
martial spirit among the men of that once proud country?

The program of the Dilutionists was fraught with danger for the whole of Grand Fenwick, and far from ensuring its survival must, in the long run, bring about its downfall.

After some more discussion, much of it heated, but no progress toward the solution of the vital problem, the two sides turned to the throne for a ruling in the matter, and the duchess faced the first crisis of her reign.

"Bobo," she said to Mountjoy, forgetting the formality of the occasion and calling him by his pet name, "what do other nations do when they are short of money? I don't mean big nations, but little ones like ours?"

"They issue a new but limited series of stamps which are bought at high prices by stamp collectors all over the world."

"We have already issued so many series of stamps," said Benter, "that they are not worth the money printed on the face of them. It has got to the point where it actually costs us more to issue the stamps than we can expect to receive in return."

"I read the other day," said the duchess, "that the Americans are giving away millions to lots of countries and not even asking for the money back. Can't we arrange to get a loan of some kind from the United States?"

"They are only giving the money away to countries they are afraid might become Communist, your Grace," replied Benter. "Nobody in Grand Fenwick would ever become a Communist. We all work our own lands. We know how hard it is to make a little profit. Nobody can call himself oppressed. Unless a man suspects that others are getting more than their fair share, there is no reason for him to become a Communist."

"Couldn't we organize a Communist party here—just for the purpose of obtaining a loan?" Gloriana asked. "I don't really mean that we want a true Communist party— just someone who would stand up and tell the people to unite against oppression and throw off their shackles and all those other things. Then we could arrange for the matter to be reported in the American newspapers. An American senator could be invited over and could see some mass meetings. They'd have to be held on Sundays because everybody is busy during the week. But we could get a dispensation from the bishop for holding a political meeting on Sunday. Then the American senator could report to Washington and we could persuade him to recommend a loan to save the duchy from Communism."

To her surprise it was David Benter, Dilutionist leader and acknowledged spokesman of the working class, who raised the strongest objection to the plan which took the rest of the delegates completely by surprise. He came of sturdy yeoman stock, and one of his ancestors had accompanied Sir Roger Fenwick when the castle in which they were now sitting was stormed and the duchy founded.

"My lady," he said, shaking his big head solemnly, "it will not do. Even if we obtained the loan, we could not pay back the money and so would forfeit some of our independence by being in the debt of another nation. Your ancestors and mine, your Highness, fought to make this an independent country. It is not a big one. But it is as free as any in the world, and has been free longer than most. It would not be right to lose any of that freedom now. Our forefathers passed liberty on to us with the land we were born in, and it is the part of free men to pass the same liberty on to their children, though we all must live in rags to do it."

"But Americans never take over any of the lands of the nations they lend money to, nor do they insist upon getting the money back," said Mountjoy. "They are quite different from any other people in the world in this respect. For some reason, which I don't understand, they are content with their own country and don't want anybody else's. So we would be in no danger if we borrowed a large sum from them to save Grand Fenwick from Communism. I move that we accept the suggestion from the throne and organize a Communist party for the purpose of obtaining money from the United States of America."

There was an hour more of debate before Mountjoy could get the matter put to a vote. The division found six in favor of the proposal and four against it and the motion was carried.

"Now," said the duchess, pleased at the success of her first test in the position of leader of her people, "who shall we get to be chief of the Communists?"

"It must be some one from Grand Fenwick," said Benter solemnly. "You can't trust those foreign Communists at all. They have no patriotism even for the place that they come from."

"We could ask Tully Bascomb," said Mountjoy. "He is always against everything, and might be persuaded to be for Communism and against Grand Fenwick if we convinced him that he was really for Grand Fenwick and against Communism. I humbly submit that the leader of the Dilutionist party and myself form a bipartisan delegation of two to persuade him that he can show no higher patriotism to Grand Fenwick than becoming a Communist and advocating the overthrow of the nation."

The Duchess Gloriana XII put a pretty finger to her pretty cheek in deep thought.

"No," she said. "On so delicate a mission as this, I believe I should go myself. You and Mr. Benter might be too successful and make a real Communist out of Mr. Bascomb."

2

TULLY BASCOMB LIVED IN A SMALL AND SECLUDED COTTAGE
on the outskirts of Fenwick Forest. It was two miles
from the City of Fenwick which clustered around the
castle and in which most of the duchy's subjects lived.

The forest was a national preserve. Perhaps it is really
too much to call it a forest, for it comprised no more than
five hundred acres, so that anyone who was not from
Grand Fenwick would call it a wood, or perhaps even a
copse.

But Grand Fenwick was as proud of its five hundred
wooded acres as if it were as large and as varied as the
redwood forests of California. The forest had indeed all
the features of far more imposing preserves. It counted
fifty different varieties of trees, a waterfall twenty feet
high, a haunted oak where a mad huntsman had hanged
himself, and three miles of walks and paths which were
really the same walk and path winding around within a
few feet of itself, each portion carefully concealed from
the rest by trees and bushes.

Tully Bascomb was the chief forest ranger of Grand
Fenwick. The title suggests a staff of forest rangers of
lower degree, and, indeed, he had a staff of one—his
father, Pierce Bascomb. The two had lived together on
the outskirts of the forest for the whole of Tully's twenty-
eight years, the father resigning the post of chief forest
ranger in favor of his son, both to provide him with employment and to insure the preservation of the forest
when he died.

The elder Bascomb, bespectacled, tall, and lean, with
eyebrows so bushy that they more than compensated for
the lack of a vestige of hair on his pate, was among
Grand Fenwick's most distinguished citizens. He was the
only living author in the whole duchy, which boasted but

two authors in all its history. His *Migratory Birds of Grand Fenwick* was held to be a work of the greatest learning, and had been published by popular subscription, while his *Grand Fenwick Birds of Prey* and *Fenwickian Songbirds* were reckoned works the equal of anything published in Europe.

Some quibble had once been raised by an American ornithologist that a nation no more than five miles long and three wide could hardly claim to have any native birds. All, he had been bold enough to assert, must be birds which came from other countries, stopping in Grand Fenwick only for a short while on their way to other places. To this Pierce Bascomb had replied, in a paper addressed to the Audubon Society and published by them, that the only being who could claim to pass with authority on the nationality of a bird was the bird itself. On the same basis it might be argued that there were no British birds and no American birds, although innumerable books had been written, published and generally accepted which assigned the nationality of these two countries to the bird life to be found in them.

That being so, Grand Fenwick could claim to have a native bird life with the same amount of justice as any other nation, however large it might be. The discussion was thereupon dropped and Pierce Bascomb's books on the bird life of Grand Fenwick accepted.

Nor was this the sum total of the achievements of the great literary man of the duchy. He had also published three books dealing with the flora of the nation, and although the total circulation of all his works was less than five thousand copies, he was, next to the Duchess Gloriana XII, Grand Fenwick's most revered and beloved citizen.

His son, Tully, however, though widely quoted and regarded as the philosopher and wit of the country, was not held in the same esteem as his father. Partially this was due to the fact he had no respect for anyone's opinion, not even his own. He had but to hear a statement to deny it, or if not deny it, at least demand that it be examined scrupulously to see whether it was true or false.

Also he was of a roving nature. He had not only been to
France and to Switzerland, but even to Italy and England and twice to the United States of America. And
all this journeying, far beyond the means of the richest
of citizens, he had accomplished without a penny in his
pocket.

He would turn the charge of the national forest over
to his father and, with no more credit in the world than
a quick tongue and a suit of clothes, leave for some distant part for a month, six months or even a year or two.

Anyone who left Grand Fenwick to live abroad even
for a short while was suspected of lacking loyalty to his
homeland, although he might achieve some esteem as a
traveler, and there had at one time been a movement to
exclude Tully altogether from the country as unworthy
to be a citizen. Only the eminence of his father prevented
the movement from succeeding, but his position was still
one of half citizen and half alien.

All these things the Duchess Gloriana XII thought of
as she rode her ducal bicycle from the castle to Tully's
cottage on the fringes of the forest. She herself could not
make up her mind whether she liked Tully or she didn't.
Partially, she had to admit, this was the reason why she
had elected to see him about the Communist proposal instead of entrusting the matter to the Count of Mountjoy
and Benter. It would be a good opportunity for finding
out exactly what she did feel about him.

He was not physically her ideal of a man, she told
herself. He had his father's bushy eyebrows and a rather
prominent nose. He was tall and tended to stoop and
his limbs seemed to be at odds with each other, as if
his frame had been constructed of assorted joints not
one of which was the mate to the other. Also he had a
most impolite way of looking you straight in the eyes as
if searching for a hidden motive in even the most innocent conversation. And thinking of this, the duchess decided that she would come straight to the point in her
interview with Tully.

She found him in the kitchen of the cottage, a leather

apron around his waist, soling a pair of stout boots at a cobbler's last. He rose as she entered, beckoned her to a chair with his hammer, and then took a handful of nails out of his mouth.

"I was expecting you, your Grace," he said when she was seated. "What can I do for you?"

"What do you mean you were expecting me?" Gloriana demanded, coloring a little with pique. "Did somebody tell you I was coming?"

"No. But the last election was a draw between the Dilutionists and the Anti-Dilutionists. It is quite impossible for a democracy to work without one side imposing its will on the other. So although you have popular representation, in its truest form, you haven't got a government. In such circumstances it is usual for someone to form a third party, drawing on voters from both sides. The thing has been going on in France for so long that nobody can say what any particular party stands for. The next step is usually a dictatorship. I presume you want me to form a third party."

Gloriana was so taken aback and indeed hurt at being anticipated in this manner that for a minute she couldn't say anything. She felt cheated. She had wanted to surprise Tully with the plan to form a third party and he had taken the whole éclat of the thing away by telling her of it himself. She decided there and then that she was sure she didn't like him.

"Well," she said at last, "that's perfectly true. I do want you to form a third party. But I don't want it to be a successful party. At least, I don't want it to be really successful, but only to appear successful. You see, we're short of money."

"Who isn't," said Tully. "As you see, I was mending my own shoes when you called, though it's so interesting a job, now I know how, that I don't know why anybody should pay someone else to do the work. If your Grace is in need of the services of a cobbler, I will be completely happy to place myself at your disposal as perhaps cobbler extraordinary to the duchy of Grand Fenwick."

"This is nothing to joke about," said Gloriana sharply. "It's serious. Grand Fenwick needs money. There are too many people here now to be supported by our own products. So we have to import food and clothing. And we have to have money to do that. Mr. Benter believes we can make enough by adding water to the Pinot to increase our exports of wine. But Count Mountjoy says that would spoil the market for the wine and be disastrous in the long run.

"That's why we want you to form a third party. We want you to form a Communist party. Hold a meeting next Sunday—we can get permission from Bishop Alvin —and tell people that the government must be overthrown, and so on. Then we will tell the Americans that the government is threatened by Communist infiltration and they will lend us all the money we need."

Tully had been lighting his pipe during this explanation, for outside of official meetings in the castle formality was dropped in Grand Fenwick in the presence of the duchess. This was not through lack of respect, but because if formalities were insisted upon half a day's work might be lost if she decided to take a tour of the country. And she couldn't be expected to remain locked up in the castle all day in the interests of maintaining production.

Tully's match went out in his hand, he was so interested in what Gloriana was saying.

"Communist party!" he exclaimed. "But Communism wouldn't work here. It's a philosophy completely unsuited to agricultural areas. You can force poor beggars in factories to produce more products, but a farmer can't force the land to produce. He can't preach Marx to the weather so that it rains at the right time. And in the whole of Russia the sun has never been known for as much as one day to listen to the economics of the late Joseph Stalin. Communism could never make any headway in Grand Fenwick."

"I'm very glad to hear it," retorted Gloriana smugly, "because as I said, I don't want it to be successful. We just want it to appear successful so that the Americans will lend us the money we need."

"Besides," continued Tully as if he had not heard her last remark, "I don't like Communism. I don't like to think that anyone's my equal. Nobody is. I'm superior to a great number of people and inferior to others, and for that reason I'm not at all sure that I'm in favor of democracy either. It's nonsense to have the vote of someone who only after enormous struggle achieves the ability to read be the equal of the vote of another who can read in twenty-four languages, though reading is no criterion. I merely cite it as an example."

By this time the duchess had completely lost sight of the main topic. "Just what kind of a government do you favor?" she asked.

"I'm not sure," said Tully. "I toyed with anarchy once, but on reading into the subject found that there were as many kinds of anarchy as there are of democracy. There are plain anarchists and syndicalist anarchists, and deviationist anarchists and, for all I know, syndicalist deviationist anarchists. There's as much anarchy in anarchy as there is in any political philosophy. But I'm still looking around."

"Well, while you're looking around, wouldn't you like trying to be a Communist for a while? Even if you don't like it, remember that it's for your country. It's an act of patriotism to help us survive. We have as much right to survive as bigger nations have. We have been a free nation for about six hundred years and hundreds of thousands of people have been born and grown up and died happily in Grand Fenwick. Just because we are a little nation doesn't mean that we should surrender our own liberty and our own pride and all our traditions and heritages and unite with some other country in order to live. It's not our fault that we haven't got any money. We've lived courageously and honorably for six centuries, but times have changed against us." She was not too far from tears when she finished.

Tully looked at her softly, almost with devotion, which was something he extended to no one but his father. "You really love Grand Fenwick, don't you?" he asked gently.

"Yes," replied the duchess, "and so does everyone here. It is our earth and our air. You do too, don't you?"

Tully walked over to the window. "Sometimes," he said slowly, "in places like Seattle or London or the Black Forest in Germany when I have supposed myself happy, I have thought suddenly of this valley and those mountains, which hold their own blue mist in the evening, and my heart has become so hungry that I had to come back. It is a madness really, for all mountains have their mists and the evening voices in all valleys are the same."

"Would you love the mountains if they were part of France or Switzerland?"

"I believe I would die rather than that."

"Then I know you love Grand Fenwick. It is not just the mountains. It is the country, and the country is in danger now. Once we could survive with our longbows and our spirit of independence. But now neither are of any avail. We have to have money. Will you do what I ask and pretend to be a Communist?"

Tully turned to face her and shook his head slowly. "No," he said. "Even if I agreed to do it and the ruse was successful and we got the money, the country would not be saved. We would have sold, indeed, the better part of it, for we would have sold our honor. We as a nation would have deliberately defrauded another and generous nation, filching money from it merely because it has plenty."

He paused for a minute, tamping the tobacco in his pipe with a long forefinger. "You said that little nations have a right to survive as well as big ones," he continued. "That is true. But big and rich nations should not be victimized just because they are big and rich. Because the United States has money and to spare does not make it any less wrong to trick some of that money out of her. To rob the millionaire is as dishonorable a thing as to rob the widow. We cannot hold our head up as a nation if we have survived by fraud; we can no longer talk of national pride if we have stooped to international thievery. If by such methods we obtained enough money from the United States to make every man, woman, and child in Grand Fenwick a millionaire, they would be blackguard millionaires all guilty of selling their country's honor for their own individual survival."

"I hadn't thought of it that way," said the duchess slowly. "All I was thinking of was to get the money, so we could go on as we have in the past. Maybe you are right. But we must hit on something. Isn't there some honorable way of making ends meet?"

"There's emigration," Tully replied. "We could encourage people to leave and find work in other countries."

Gloriana shook her head. "Everybody in Grand Fenwick has a right to stay here if they want," she said. "It's their country. They shouldn't be forced to leave it to earn a living. And besides, emigration used to work, but it doesn't any longer. I read somewhere that Italy tried to solve its population problem by emigration to the United States. But now there are more people in Italy than there were before the big migrations started and all as poor as ever. And the United States is getting so full that they've established quotas. The quota they would fix for Grand Fenwick would probably be only one or two every five years. That wouldn't help. We'll have to think of something else."

They were silent for a while. Gloriana glanced at Tully and disturbed as she was by the country's economic problems, found herself thinking that there was something about this man that set him off from and indeed above his fellows. He was of the common clay, but the common clay in a different mold. His face was turned halfway from her, the head held up, and with a start she caught, for just a second, a remarkable resemblance between Tully Bascomb and the portrait of her ancestor Sir Roger Fenwick in the castle of the duchy. He turned towards her and the likeness was gone.

"There's only one method of getting money from another nation that is recognized by tradition as honorable," Tully said solemnly.

"What is that?" asked the duchess, with a strange feeling that at this moment she was talking, not to a contemporary man, but to Sir Roger Fenwick himself.

Tully walked over to the chimney and chose from several standing there a six-foot bow stave of yew.

"War," he said.

"War!" echoed Gloriana in astonishment.

"War," repeated Tully. "We could declare war on the United States."

3

DUCHESS GLORIANA SELECTED A POMEGRANATE FROM A
dish of fruit before her and could not suppress, even
on so solemn an occasion as a meeting of her Privy
Council, a smile of anticipation. Pomegranates were her
favorite fruit. They were a little hard to come by in
Grand Fenwick, and her father, the duke, had during
his lifetime limited her to pomegranates at Christmas
and on her birthday. But now, since she was the duchess, she could have them whenever she wanted.

"Bobo," she said, picking up a silver fruit knife and
turning to the Count of Mountjoy, "how long is it since
we went to war?"

"A little over five hundred years," replied the count.
He thought it an idle question, posed by a curious and
somewhat willful girl, who also happened to be his
sovereign lady. Just what the Privy Council meeting had
been summoned for he was not sure. But he prided himself on knowledge of the history of his country and took
this opportunity of airing it. "The occasion," he continued, "was a war with France, and the battle was
fought in the Pass of Pinot. There were four hundred
and thirty under the double-headed eagle of Fenwick—
four hundred bowmen and thirty men at arms. An ancestor of yours, my lady, and one of mine, were among
those on the field. The French numbered twelve hundred. They made three charges down the pass, in
bodies of four hundred knights to each charge, and
were met with the arrows of Grand Fenwick, loosed
with such discipline and courage that at the end of the
day, seven hundred of the French were dead, and our
losses amounted to only five."

"No other war since then?" asked the duchess, busy
with the little ruby beads of the pomegranate.

"None," said the count. His silver head, illumined by the sunlight, looked not unlike that of the eagle which was the national emblem. "None have been necessary. The battle of the Pass of Pinot settled for all time the sovereignty and right to respect and freedom of the duchy of Grand Fenwick."

"We must be badly out of practice—I mean at fighting wars," murmured the duchess.

"Perhaps," replied the count. "But should the necessity arise again, I have no doubt that we would give a good account of ourselves. Indeed, the contest would be most interesting. Our national weapon, the longbow, has been out of date for so long that it has become, in many ways, a super weapon. It can kill at a range of five hundred yards. It is completely accurate in skilled hands. It is silent. It requires a low expenditure for ammunition, and lends itself excellently to mass fire."

"I'm very glad to hear all this," replied the duchess, delicately putting aside the remains of her pomegranate, "because we will have to go to war again quite soon."

"The longbow," continued the count, "is an example of a weapon which, like the mace—excuse me. What was that, your Highness? Did I hear you say that we will have to go to war again quite soon?"

"Just so," said Gloriana.

The count allowed his monocle to fall into his lap. "Your Highness is not serious?" he suggested hopefully.

"We are," replied the duchess.

"Why," said the count, "this is an utterly ridiculous proposal. It is monstrous. It is not to be thought upon for a moment. Are you sure, your Grace, that you are feeling well?"

"Quite well," replied Gloriana. "And if you will see if Mr. Benter is outside so we can complete the membership of the Privy Council, I will tell you all about it."

There was no mistaking that this last was an order, coming from a ruler to a subject, and despite his astonishment which gave him a sense of having been mentally paralyzed for the moment, the count rose to bring in the leader of the Dilutionist party. He was gone some little while—longer than the courtesies of the court would permit in normal circumstances—and when he returned with Mr. Benter, both were agitated and worried.

"Gentlemen," said Gloriana, eying the pomegranates but deciding against them, in view of the serious nature of the business ahead. "I have called this meeting for two purposes. The first is to report to you as the leaders of the two principal parties of Grand Fenwick on the result of the suggestion that we form a Communist party in the duchy to obtain money from the Americans. The second is to ask your further advice—indeed, I would put the matter more strongly and say to request your assent, to an alternative course of action."

In her official occasions, the Duchess Gloriana XII showed a marked ability to shift from young woman to distant sovereign. This, her newly elected party leaders were just beginning to discover and they found the tactic overwhelming. A few moments before, the duchess had been a rather ingenuous girl, picking on a pomegranate. Now she was the ruler of a nation, intent upon wielding her authority.

"As to the proposal for the formation of a Communist party," she continued, "you will recall that I undertook myself to put the matter to Tully Bascomb, who it was agreed would be the best and safest person to lead such an organization. However, he was able to persuade me that this was the wrong course of action."

Count Mountjoy exchanged a surprised look with Benter.

"He pointed out that even if the plan were successful and the money obtained from the United States, Grand Fenwick would be guilty of perpetrating an international fraud which would besmirch the honorable record we have maintained over so many centuries."

"But, your Highness," interposed Mountjoy, "we cannot feed our people on honor. If it is a choice between honor and want, between spiritual or physical survival, then the material things must come first. Man did not discover he had a soul until he was well fed, with prospects of that condition continuing for some time. Hungry people cannot afford honor and hungry nations cannot indulge in too nice manners."

"You're wrong there," said Benter. "I'm beginning to like that man Tully, though in the past I found him too contrary for comfort. To my way of thinking neither men nor nations can survive without keeping their self-respect."

"Precisely what Bascomb himself had to say," said Gloriana. "In any case, he refused to form a Communist party because he said he didn't agree with Communism, and from what I could gather he didn't agree with democracy either. In fact, he wasn't quite sure what he did agree with."

"We had better get back to watering the wine," interposed Benter. "It is the only way out of our difficulties. And there is nothing dishonorable about it. There is no statement on the Grand Fenwick label as to what is the water content in the bottle."

"You will ruin the major source of revenue of the country if you do," rejoined Mountjoy with some heat.

"I don't believe either of you are right," said Gloriana.

"Perhaps Mr. Bascomb had a solution to propose?" asked Mountjoy with more than a trace of sarcasm.

"That is precisely why I called this meeting," replied Gloriana. "Mr. Bascomb has got a solution which will provide us with the money we need from the United States and leave our national honor unbesmirched." She paused to give emphasis to what was to follow.

"Mr. Bascomb," she said, separating each word distinctly from the next, "has convinced me that we should declare war on the United States."

For the second time that morning Count Mountjoy dropped his monocle. Mr. Benter gave a little start, as if he had been dozing and someone had poked him hard in the back with a finger.

"Go to war with the United States?" he said in such disbelief that he seemed scarcely able to credit having heard the appalling words.

"Go to war with the United States?" echoed the count, so profoundly shocked that he had not yet replaced his monocle, without which he was wont to maintain, no man could claim to be fully dressed.

"Go to war with the United States," repeated Gloriana grimly, evenly and indeed with a savor of approval.

The count shuddered. He picked up his monocle and put it in place, as if this gesture, by some special magic of its own, might help restore the world to sanity. He smoothed his silver hair with long fingers that trembled slightly. He so far forgot himself as to wet his lips with the tip of his tongue.

"The man's mad," he said at last. "Completely bereft of his senses. He's dangerous. Talk like that could result in the most serious trouble. Reported in certain sections of the United States press, it might arouse such popular feelings against us as to cost us the greater part of our American market for Pinot. If that should happen, we might as well go to war with the United States indeed, or with the whole world, for that matter. For all would be lost anyway. Bascomb, your Highness, should be locked up for a raving lunatic. He has been at large too long."

Benter was inclined to agree. The unparalleled proposal, so calmly presented by the ruler of the duchy, had robbed him for a while of his ability to as much as frame a thought, let alone say a word. But the denunciations of the opposition, represented by the count, had loosed his tongue, and he was now intensely curious to know the reason why such a remarkable plan had been advanced.

"Your Grace," he said when the count had calmed down, "what advantage did Bascomb believe we could reap from a declaration of war against the Americans?"

"He said that traditionally war was the only way in which one nation, in need of money and without the credit to borrow any, could obtain it from another."

"That may be so," said Benter, still quite at a loss. "But there are a lot more things to be thought of. First there's the outcome of the war. The population of the

United States is around one hundred and sixty million, I believe. Ours is but six thousand. Then the United States has great fleets of ships and airplanes, masses of tanks and heavy guns, small arms by the millions and all kinds, and, to cap everything, an unknown quantity of atomic and hydrogen bombs. We have only longbows, spears and maces. And the biggest army we could raise would be only a thousand men and boys. It is hardly necessary to say that we would lose this war just as soon as we started it."

"Hardly necessary to say it at all," agreed the duchess serenely. "I am quite aware that we would lose the war."

"Then what would be the reason for fighting it?" persisted Benter.

The duchess leaned back in her chair, feeling nicely superior at the thought that she had the leaders of the two political parties of Grand Fenwick completely mystified. She picked up the silver fruit knife and felt the blade with a pretty finger.

"The Americans," she said, almost as if musing aloud to herself, "are a strange people. They do not behave like other nations in any way. In fact, in many ways, they behave exactly the opposite of other nations. Where other countries rarely forgive anything, the Americans will forgive everything. Where others rarely forget a wrong, the Americans rarely remember one. Indeed, they are so quick to forgive and forget that there is almost a race in their minds which to do first."

"That is perhaps quite true, your Grace," said Benter, "but I do not see that it has anything to do with our declaring war on the United States and being defeated by them."

"That," replied the duchess with a smile of mild rebuke, "is because you have not paid much attention to history; and you, Count Mountjoy, have become an expert on the history of Grand Fenwick to the exclusion of that of other nations. The fact is that there are few more profitable undertakings for a country in need of money than to declare war on the United States and be

THE MOUSE THAT ROARED

defeated. Hardly an acre of land is forfeited in such wars.

"It is usually agreed, to be sure, that heavy industries and other installations and activities which could be used in future wars are to be dismantled, destroyed and their reestablishment banned. And it usually evolves that this is not done, because it is decided that to follow such a plan would either wreck the economy of the defeated nation, or make it incapable of defending itself against other foes. In either or both cases, the Americans would feel called upon, such is their peculiar nature, to help out at their own expense.

"Again, it is usually decided that the nation and people which lose to the United States shall be made to suffer national and individual hardship for the aggression. And the ink is no sooner dry on such agreements than the United States is rushing food, machinery, clothing, money, building materials and technical aid for the relief of its former foes.

"Once more, it is always laid down that the defeated armies must be disbanded and never again be allowed to reform. But, a little later, it is discovered that these armies are in an oblique but nonetheless definite manner essential to the security of the United States itself. Either the defeated enemy must have an army and navy and air force of its own, or the Americans must remain there in an indefinite occupation.

"Americans, particularly American soldiers, do not like to remain long outside their own country. And in a matter of months, or at the most years, the United States is first requesting and then begging its former enemies to raise an army to defend their own territory. It is not unheard of that these defeated foes are able to state the terms under which they will raise an army for their own policing and defense. Those terms have involved the payments of large sums of money by the United States, or the extension of generous credits, revision of trade agreements in favor of the defeated nation, return of shipping, rehabilitation of factories destroyed in the war, and even the gift of the equipment needed for the army.

"All in all, as I said before, there is no more profitable and sound step for a nation without money or credit to take, than declare war on the United States and suffer a total defeat." She smiled indulgently at the two of them.

Count Mountjoy, who had commenced listening to the discourse as if he were hearing a sentence of doom pronounced, was, when it ended, filled with lively interest.

"Why," he exclaimed, "the plan has possibilities that border on brilliant. We declare war on Monday, are vanquished Tuesday, and rehabilitated beyond our wildest dreams by Friday night. I must confess that I misjudged Bascomb completely. The man is gifted with flashes of purest genius."

"This is not completely Bascomb's plan," Gloriana cautioned slyly. "The being defeated part is mine. His proposal is that we attack the United States—and win."

"A madman," said the count sadly. "A madman."

"But," continued the duchess, "there is no reason why we should not let him continue in his madness since we know in advance what the outcome will be."

"None at all," commented Mountjoy happily.

"I think we are going too fast," interrupted Benter. "There are still some things that I do not understand. If Bascomb is, and rightly in my opinion, so anxious about preserving the international honor and standing of the duchy, what grounds, other than lack of money, does he offer for going to war? To declare war on a peace-loving state, even a big one, without good reason is nothing more than barbarism."

"Oh, he has a good reason—or rather, we have," the duchess replied. "Indeed, we have a reason which must, if it becomes known, swing world sympathy to our side."

"What is that?"

"United States aggression against the duchy of Grand

Fenwick." She rang a heavy bell on the table before her and the court chamberlain entered discreetly.

"Bring in the bottle," the duchess commanded.

He was gone only a minute and returned with a bottle of familiar size, color and proportions.

"Look at the label," Gloriana said, placing the bottle before them. They looked and read, with growing horror, the words:

PINOT GRAND ENWICK
The Wine of Connoisseurs

There was a picture of the castle of Grand Fenwick and the label was in every way similar to that used on their own precious wine. But at the bottom, in type so small as to be almost invisible, was the phrase:

Product of San Rafael, Calif., U.S.A.

"The dogs," cried Mountjoy, leaping to his feet and flinging back his chair. "Rich as they are, with abundance on every hand, they still seek to deprive us of our only source of livelihood. For a few dollars more for themselves they would beggar every man, woman, and child in Grand Fenwick. They shall pay heavily for this."

The vote, both in the Privy Council and subsequently in the Council of Freemen, to declare war on the United States of America was unanimous.

4

CHET BESTON, CORRESPONDENCE CLERK FOR THE CENTRAL
European Division of the United States Department of
State, decided that the time had come for him to start
taking some exercise again. He was a man in his mid-
thirties with an active and not undistinguished career
behind him. He had been graduated from Columbia
with a major in political science and a minor in jour-
nalism just in time to join the army at the outbreak of
World War II.

His professors had advised him to apply for some
special position in the armed services in view of his
university background. But a sincere and deep patriotism had convinced Chet that there would be something
morally wrong in doing this. It would look like asking
for special favors, a place of security and safety for himself, when his country needed every fighting man who
could be mustered. So he started as a private in an in-
fantry regiment, went to sergeant, volunteered as a
paratrooper and eventually joined the Office of Strategic Services, making several secret parachute drops
in the Balkans on special missions.

The end of the war found him with more than his
quota of decorations, a love of exercise and nowhere
to go. His background suggested the diplomatic service
and resulted in his appointment as clerk in the Central
European Division of the Department of State.

"There is no substitute for learning any business from
the ground up, son," said Senator Griffin, who helped
him to the post. "Learn all you can about those foreign-
ers—but especially keep your eye on our own men. It
takes three years for an alien, resident in the United
States, to become an American citizen; but it takes only six
months for a citizen, resident in the State Department,

to become an alien. Report anything you find to me."

Chet hadn't found anything except that he didn't have to work very hard or know too much to keep his job. He found himself developing what he called a State Department jog—a kind of preoccupied, learned, but not unkindly shuffle down the corridors from office to office. He found too that this was about the only exercise he got. So today he decided that he would go down to Georgetown, pick up a canoe and paddle it a couple of miles up and down the Potomac to tone him up.

He was just at the point of leaving his office when a messenger came by and threw a long and impressive envelope on his desk.

"What's cooking?" Chet asked by way of being friendly. He felt sorry for the messenger, who had been padding around the State Department for twenty years. Sometimes he thought of him as a sort of captive, a trustee in a huge diplomatic prison.

"Nothing much," the messenger replied. "The boys in the pressroom are up to their usual tricks. That's about all." He nodded and padded out and Chet picked up the envelope. There were some heavy, old-fashioned seals on it which was unusual and made him think for a moment that this was something special. But when he opened the envelope, he started chuckling.

At the top was a double-headed eagle crest, the eagle saying, "Yea" from one beak and "Nay" from the other. Below, in Old English lettering, was the title *"Duchy Of Grand Fenwick."* The message, written in an impressive cursive script, read:

> To the President, Congress and People of the United States of America—Greetings.

> WHEREAS, The duchy of Grand Fenwick has been a sovereign and independent nation since its founding in 1370 A.D.; and
> WHEREAS, It is thus in a position to treat on equal terms with other sovereign and independent nations, this right having been recognized among civilized communities for over five centuries; and

WHEREAS, The principal support of the people of the duchy of Grand Fenwick has been during all these years, the production of the excellent and unique wine known to the world as Pinot Grand Fenwick, which is pressed from the grapes of ancient vineyards on the southern slopes of the northern mountains of the duchy; and

WHEREAS, An ignoble imitation of this superior wine, under the name of Pinot Grand Enwick, is being produced in quantity and sold at a fifth of the cost by certain wineries in the city of San Rafael in the State of California, which is part of the geographical and political territory of the United States of America; and

WHEREAS, The sale of this spurious product threatens the livelihood of the independent duchy of Grand Fenwick; and

WHEREAS, Repeated representations demanding that this injustice be remedied have been ignored by the ministries and government of the United States: therefore be it

Resolved, That the duchy of Grand Fenwick holds the sale of this wine an unwarranted and unjust and persistent and planned action of aggression against the duchy; therefore be it

Resolved, The duchy of Grand Fenwick, having taken all steps it can to remedy the matter peaceably, does here and now, and by these presents, declare that a state of war exists between itself and the United States of America.

SIGNED:

Gloriana XII
DUCHESS OF GRAND FENWICK

D. Benter
LEADER, DILUTIONIST PARTY

Mountjoy
LEADER, ANTI-DILUTIONIST PARTY

Chet read the document through twice, chuckling now and then. "Those reporters go to a lot of trouble to have a little fun," he said. "Bunch of characters." He put the missive in his jacket pocket and set out for his canoeing. He was a little out of practice and the canoe overturned, and the document got thoroughly wet. When he got home, he put it down behind the radiator in his apartment to dry, and forgot about it.

The outfitting of the Grand Fenwick Expeditionary Force for the attack on the United States proved a far more complicated matter than the duchess or either of her party leaders had anticipated. Count Mountjoy had hoped that no expeditionary force would be necessary. A declaration of war, he thought secretly, would be sufficient. It could be followed immediately by an appeal to the world, then a quick surrender, and then the wonderful rehabilitation by the United States would commence.

But the declaration of war had been followed by four weeks of ominous silence from the United States. Any reply would have been welcome. None at all was intolerable. He did not mention his fears to the duchess, but he got into a habit of watching the sky under the growing conviction that an atom bomb was to be expected at any moment, without even the chance of surrendering first. There was no United States representative in Grand Fenwick whom he could consult, and in the end he had obtained the permission of the duchess to visit the nearest American consulate in France to inquire for an answer.

He had been met with smiles and chuckles. Everybody there seemed to regard the whole thing as a joke. It was mortifying to have to report to Gloriana that the United States' reaction to Grand Fenwick's solemn declaration of war had been a guffaw of laughter from the consul, a clap upon the back and an inquiry as to whether he had heard the one about the man who had bet a hundred dollars he could solve any charade presented him.

It was only at this point that it was decided to get together an expeditionary force and start the war in earnest. Tully Bascomb was appointed high constable of the Fenwick Army for the duration of hostilities and told to raise the men needed for an attack upon the United States.

He entered the project with vigor, deciding that a force of three men at arms besides himself and twenty longbow-men would be sufficient. An ancient law of the duchy, demanding that in case of war all able-bodied men present themselves at the castle armed and equipped according to their degree, was invoked. On the day appointed, seven hundred turned up with bows, quivers of arrows, small round shields, short swords, maces, spears, leather jerkins and some with hauberks, or garments of chain mail, covering head, neck, and shoulders.

The war indeed was popular in Grand Fenwick, for the whole nation was outraged at the action of the California vintner who threatened their market and the reputation of their wine by producing a cheap imitation. All wanted to join the army and avenge the insult to their product, to their own skill and that of their forefathers. "Preserve our Pinot" became the popular cry and "Freedom from Fraud" the high ideal for which the war was to be fought to a victorious conclusion. Children as well as adults caught the war spirit and toddled in martial bands down the roads of the duchy, small bows in their hands and pots upon their heads to take the place of helmets.

With such enthusiasm, it was hard for Tully to select the twenty-three men, other than himself, needed for the expeditionary force. He decided on an elimination contest and picked twenty husky bowmen who proved that they could split a hazel wand with an arrow at five hundred paces. The three men at arms were easier to choose, for there were but twenty in the duchy who had the right to carry spears and maces, and these agreed to lots being cast.

Then came a period of severe training for the army of Grand Fenwick. All were made to climb mountains in full equipment, to cross and recross and cross again the icy river, to loose their arrows singly, by volley and in exact rotation, and, divided into two bands, to seek each other in the dark and wage battle. But in the end all was ready, and Tully reported the expeditionary force at peak training and prepared for the invasion of the American continent.

Nobody, however, and least of all the duchess, had considered how they were to get there. Gloriana had left it up to the political leaders of the government to make the arrangements, and they had left it up to Tully as high constable. So when he presented himself to report that he was ready to start the active war there was considerable embarrassment in the Privy Council.

"Surely," said Count Mountjoy, who was getting uneasier about atomic bombs with the passing of each day, and sincerely hoped that the declaration of war would not annoy the United States—"surely, it is not necessary for us to go to the expense of sending our forces across the Atlantic Ocean to attack the Americans. We must remember that we are fighting this war to get money, not to spend it. An attack on the American consulate in Lyons would be sufficient. There is a bus there every day which would be cheaper than sending the men by rail."

Tully gave him a look of such contempt that it might have been compared to a blow across the face with a glove of mail.

"You are ready for any man to lay down his life for his country provided it doesn't cost more than two shillings a head," he said. "You would attack a defenseless United States consulate and pretend you have attacked an armed nation. Do you think that the army of Grand Fenwick is the equivalent of a mob of students protesting the firing of a popular professor? We have declared war; we have declared war in an honorable cause. And we must, with honor, bring that war home to the enemy."

"Perhaps," suggested Mr. Benter, who himself was worried about the expense, "it would be possible to raise enough money through a special tax to send our forces to America on a tourist liner. They could travel third class and we could select a ship of a neutral nation."

"And how do you suppose the army of Grand Fenwick is going to get through customs and immigration when it arrives?" retorted Tully with fine irony. "You do not propose that we be carted off to Ellis Island, lock, stock and barrel, without striking a blow, do you? Or perhaps you think the United States is generous enough to issue us all visas for the purpose of landing legally and attacking the nation?"

"I was only trying to be helpful," replied Benter subdued. "We are in this war, as you say, and I will see it through to the end. If you have any reasonable suggestion to make, you may be sure of my support."

"There is only one way to get to America since we lack ships of our own and that is to charter one," Tully replied. "We could hire a small merchant vessel to take the expeditionary force over and bring it back again. As a matter of honor it would have to display the colors of Grand Fenwick. We can't sail under another flag. The captain must be completely subject to my authority as to where the force is to be landed."

"Do you know of any such ship?" Gloriana asked.

"Yes," replied Tully. "The last time I went to America it was as a seaman on board a brig sailing from Marseilles and bound for Nova Scotia. Her name was *Endeavor*, a highly suitable name for our mission. And I believe she may be had at a reasonable sum. The alternative is to tell the people of the duchy that we are calling the war off because we cannot get to the United States. I do not think that such a course of action would be well received."

Nobody had any other suggestion to offer and it was agreed to charter the *Endeavor*. A special tax of a penny on each glass of wine drunk in the duchy would pay the cost. Indeed, so popular was the cause, that the consumption of wine in Grand Fenwick during the next two weeks set a record for any time in the history of the duchy.

Finally the morning arrived for the expeditionary force to leave. They were mustered in the courtyard of the castle. At their head stood Tully, splendid in a suit of mail which gleamed in the sunlight. By his side hung a broadsword, and from a staff in his hand fluttered the twin-headed eagle banner of Grand Fenwick. Behind him stood his three men at arms, each in mail and each with a sword. It was decided to dispense with lances as they would be somewhat cumbersome.

Behind them in five ranks of four men were the long-bowmen, uniformly clad in mail shirts worn over leather jerkins and buff trunk hose, their six-foot bows slung across their backs, their bucklers on their bare arms and their quivers bristling with arrows.

Gloriana reviewed the men before they left, and reminded them that though the odds were great, yet their forefathers had met and defeated odds of a hundred to one. "You will not fight alone," she said, "for gathered around your banner will be the spirits of all those countless legions who before you struck a blow for their native land. They amount to a mighty host which will make each of you the equivalent of a thousand. If you should die, it will be but to join the bravest company of men—those who died in a similar cause before you. If you live, it will be to attain such honor as will make you the envy of your fellows, remembered in their toasts and held with warmth and reverence in their hearts. Strike hard then for your country, remembering that each shaft loosed ensures the freedom of your land." She glanced at Tully and caught again, as he saluted her with his sword, the same resemblance to Sir Roger Fenwick which had surprised her before. For a second the sun seemed more splendid upon him, and he the manliest of all men.

There was the beat of a kettle drum and the blowing of a trumpet and the group followed Tully out of the courtyard down the hill and over the bridge to the border of the duchy. Little children lined the roads and applauded. Old men and young women marched alongside. They sang the ancient war song of Grand Fenwick, "The Crooked Stick and the Gray Goose Wing." Some cried and some cheered and all felt very brave.

Outside the border of the duchy the little army changed into civilian clothing and caught the bus to Marseilles, and the people went back to their homes.

5

THE PRESIDENT OF THE UNITED STATES SAT DOWN HEAVILY
at his desk in the Oval Room of the White House and
passed a freckled hand over his sparse hair. It was nine
in the morning and he was tired. Also he had a head-
ache which he knew better than to report to the White
House physician because it might mean one of those
long medical examinations during which his blood pressure would be taken and an electrocardiogram run and
a whole lot of other rigmarole gone through.

What he needed was a couple of aspirins and three
or four hours' sleep. He had gone short of sleep during
the night because at two in the morning, Kokintz had
called.

All Kokintz had said was, "I have completed the
project, Mr. President, and it is entirely successful." He
wasn't conscious of what he had replied. Something like
"Good," or maybe, "Swell. See you in the morning."
Then he had put down the receiver and tried to go to
sleep again. But he had been awakened by dreams of
great sheets of white heat in the middle of which were
men and women who got smaller and smaller, like
icicles in the sun, until they dwindled to little dots and
then to nothing at all.

The President picked up the telephone and said to
the operator, "Get hold of the Secretary of Defense and
Senator Griffin of the Atomic Energy Commission and
ask them to come over as soon as they can without
creating a stir. And call Dr. Kokintz as well. I want to
see him too." Then he went over to the window, put his
hands behind his back and looked over the lawn, waiting.

The Secretary of Defense and Senator Griffin reported within ten minutes. The President said, "Good

38

morning," cheerfully and waved them to chairs on each
side of the desk. He was used to appearing cheerful,
even when he felt far from it.

"I've got something for you," he said with a grin. "A
real hot one." Then, noticing the look of concern on
Senator Griffin's face, added, "Nothing political, Grif."

The Senator smiled deprecatingly, but the assurance
relaxed him. He was a small, white-haired, red-faced
man; chunky as a bulldog. He always wore a gray flan-
nel suit, decorated with a tiny red rosebud in the lapel
of his coat. He came from one of the Western states and
had a slow and soothing drawl which was at surprising
odds with his appearance. For Senator Griffin looked
habitually as though he was about to explode at any
moment into a fury of denunciation at some outrage or
another. He was really a mild man, rarely aroused, but
his choleric appearance was politically useful, for it had
quelled many an unfriendly election audience.

The Secretary of Defense, by contrast, had a vague
resemblance to a mouse. This was heightened by a habit
of putting three fingers nervously against his lower lip
whenever he was about to say something, as if he were
afraid that his words would give offense where none
was intended. The President wondered at times how
the secretary ever got up the nerve to face up to some
of the army and navy brass and tell them that a favorite
project must be scrapped. He managed very well, as a
matter of fact, though the rumor was in Washington
that he was in mortal fear of his wife. At least that was
the explanation given for his leaving his office promptly
at 5:30 every afternoon, whatever might be the business at hand.

The two were hardly seated before Dr. Kokintz arrived. He was, as usual, wearing a gray pullover and a
pair of trousers which might once have been dark gray,
but now had a green and aged look to them. His jacket
was open and rumpled. It was a sports jacket of his
own design. There was no collar or lapel, but there were
innumerable pockets all over it in which pieces of paper
and pencils could be placed. Dr. Kokintz did not like

to waste time looking for a pencil or a piece of paper. The side pockets of this jacket bulged like saddlebags on a mule. In one would be a huge pipe and an equally huge tobacco pouch. In the other would probably be his luncheon sandwich, or it might be yesterday's luncheon sandwich. When Dr. Kokintz was busy or preoccupied he often forgot to eat.

He had a sharp white face and a mass of black hair. His eyes bulged behind thick glasses of unusual magnifying power, so that he gave the impression of being some underwater creature which was peering cautiously and with some surprise up from its element.

"Good morning, Mr. President," he said. "Gentlemen." He bowed slowly and graciously to the other two. He spoke excellent English, but there was just the flavor of foreign learning of it in his inflections. It wasn't an accent. Just a little trace of not being American born.

There was an awkward little silence. A clock chimed a dulcet stroke, marking the quarter hour, and from the terrace outside there came the sharp twittering of blue jays quarreling.

"Do you ever feed the birds, Mr. President?" Dr. Kokintz asked. "A few crumbs and they are quite gay." He reached for the pocket in which he kept his sandwich.

The President smiled. "We can feed the birds later," he replied. "I have brought these gentlemen—you know of course the Secretary of Defense and Senator Griffin —so that they can hear about the project. You told me last night it was finished and successful. I want them to know the details. It is hardly necessary to say that nothing that is said here will be repeated."

"Ah yes. The project," said Dr. Kokintz, releasing his sandwich reluctantly. "Yes, it is done. It is done. That last machine for calculating the navy loaned me was a great help. With the others it would have taken two years. As it was, it took only a month. Of course, I was a year setting up the problems for the machine to solve. And I had to work in the hope that a machine capable of solving them would be invented. But that is all water under the bridge. Here it is."

With some difficulty he pulled his pipe—a massive Oompaul—out of his right-hand pocket and then extricated his copious tobacco pouch. He put the pipe in his mouth and proceeded to open the pouch so that they thought for a second he was going to smoke. But instead he inserted a finger and thumb in the pouch and brought out a dull metal cylinder, not much bigger than a bobbin. He threw it on the desk, and it rolled, with little bits of tobacco clinging to it, towards the President. The latter picked it up, weighed it in his hand, and then put it down again, one eyebrow cocked in interrogation.

"Enough," said Kokintz, "to incinerate an area of two million square miles. Perhaps more. You know how we scientists are. We cannot be sure without trying."

The other two looked at the little cylinder with mixed curiosity and awe.

The Secretary of Defense spoke first. He put his three fingers to his lower lip, looking as nervous as a schoolboy asking a question before the whole class and said, "What is it?"

"Quadium," said Kokintz. "A form of hydrogen which has not existed in the universe in billions of years. It is quite impossible to say how long. When I say that it is a form of hydrogen, you must realize that I speak for the layman." He smiled an apologetic little smile. "It is, let us say, as closely related to the hydrogen one finds in water as man is to the ape. I will not trouble you with the details of the atomic structure. It is extremely involved. The mass difference of the nucleus is the greatest yet achieved."

"Mass difference?" queried the Secretary of Defense.

"That is an indication of the force which binds the nucleus together," said Senator Griffin, with a touch of superiority. "It is a measure of the power which will be released when the nucleus is split. Right, Doctor?"

"Yes," replied Kokintz. "But if we get into the details, you will be either confused or get a wrong impression.

With the bomb known as the atom bomb—the plutonium bomb to be more exact—only about one tenth of one per cent of the plutonium employed is converted into energy. With the quadium bomb it will be possible to convert ten per cent of the quadium into energy. And the energy released is far more powerful, unit for unit, than that released with the plutonium bomb.

"To continue, this form of hydrogen, which, as I said, existed on this earth billions of years ago, is believed to have been the substance which made the earth a flaming planet with a temperature equivalent to perhaps a thousand times that of the surface of the sun. When this quadium had been completely exhausted, converted into denser nuclei, the earth still continued to flame for millions of years until it eventually cooled down, and life was formed on it.

"It was the quadium, we believe, which first set the fire. There is no quadium on the sun. That has all burned up eons ago. In fact, there is no quadium anywhere that we know of in the whole of space, other than that which is on the desk before you."

"You mean *nowhere?*" asked Senator Griffin.

"Nowhere but there," said Dr. Kokintz pointing to the tiny cylinder.

The clock struck the half hour and the noise of it frightened the blue jays, who fled across the lawn.

"What will it do?" the President asked at length.

Kokintz picked up the container, held it a few inches from his thick glasses, and put it down again with every evidence of loathing.

"It will do whatever may be the will of man in the way of destruction. It will make of the atomic bomb something comparatively as harmless as a child's toy pistol. It will give to the nation which possesses it in the form of a bomb the ability to destroy a complete continent. It will, in short, make of war a strictly one-shot affair. Indeed, there is now no foreseeable limit to the power of the explosive we can manufacture from quadium other than the amount of quadium available. We could, in theory, blow the whole of the North

American continent off the face of the earth. Perhaps South America too."

Again there was a silence interrupted only by the plodding, purposeful ticking of the clock. The President looked at it and said, "How long, in point of time, do you think we may be ahead of the others in the discovery of quadium?"

Kokintz shrugged. "Maybe five years. Maybe only two. Somewhere between there, I would say, depending upon the amount of information which has been leaked to them. I am not myself convinced that the others have even an atomic bomb, although they may have achieved an atomic explosion. However, for safety's sake, it would be best to assume that they have a workable atomic bomb. That is the first step to a quadium bomb.

"You know, of course, that there is a limit to the amount of power which can be released with an atomic bomb. The limit is set by the mass of fission material which is used. Only a certain amount will work. More than that, and the bomb will not explode. It is generally agreed that the most powerful atomic bomb that can be built would be the equivalent of a mere 150,000 tons of high explosive such as TNT."

He stopped, took off his thick glasses, put them in one of the numerous pockets of his coat and screwed up his eyelids as if his eyes were hurting him. He seemed like a man who was standing in more light than a human being should be called upon to endure. It was as if he were being shriveled by it. He hunched his shoulders and let his hands dangle before him as if they were lifeless. Then he continued.

"A deuterium bomb," he said, "which is the bomb talked of in the newspapers as the hydrogen bomb or hell bomb, can be made to produce an explosion fifty times as great as that of the most powerful atom bomb. That is to say the equivalent of 7,500,000 tons of TNT. Of that we are quite sure. The explosion could be even greater.

"Then there is the tritium bomb, for which the press

has not yet invented a name. Conservatively a tritium bomb would release a force equivalent to the spontaneous detonation of more than 22,000,000 tons of TNT. It might be a far greater force than that. I am inclined to believe it would. I am talking now, of course, in terms of the use of the same quantity of deuterium and tritium in the bombs."

"Tritium bomb?" asked the Secretary of Defense.

"Also a form of hydrogen," Kokintz explained. "Like quadium, it does not occur in nature but existed on the earth during its incandescent period. Lord Rutherford, the British physicist, produced the first samples in 1935. But they were regarded as a mere chemical curiosity— as indeed was deuterium when it was first produced under the name of heavy water. A future for deuterium not as a bomb but as an important agent in making dyes fast was predicted. Of course, in those days, we were concerned with poison gases and flame throwers rather than new types of explosives.

"The quadium bomb provides the ultimate weapon. One containing the same amount of quadium as there is in liquid form in that cylinder would have an explosive force equivalent to 100,000,000 tons of TNT. But that is a mere figure. A bomb capable of destroying a continent as big as the United States can be produced as readily as one which would destroy merely New York, Washington, Boston, and Philadelphia."

All the time he had been talking, Dr. Kokintz had remained in the curiously hunched shriveled stance of a man caught in a blinding searchlight. He relaxed now, quite suddenly, fished his glasses out of his pocket, put them on and smiled at the other three, as if his ordeal was over.

"You believe it might take the others as long as from two to five years to produce a usable quantity of this quadium?" asked the President grimly.

"I believe so," said Kokintz. "It is first of all necessary to arrive at the exact structure of the nucleus. The calculations are involved in the extreme—I, of course, had the help of the navy calculator. Then there is the designing of the apparatus and the establishing of controls. There is a great deal of radioactivity as the process develops. Two years, I believe, would be a safe estimate. Of course, we must remember that the other side has carried out exhaustive research into atomic nuclei using cosmic rays instead of cyclotrons. The cosmic ray is far more powerful as an atom-splitting agent than any cyclotrons we have invented. But the splitting process is much slower because of a number of factors. They may have stumbled upon the structure of the quadium atom—which is the first step toward the creation of the element—but I am inclined to doubt it."

"How long after they find how to produce quadium to the development of a quadium bomb?"

"That I cannot say at all. It depends on too many unknown factors. Theoretically the bomb is quite simple to make. The quadium will not explode until subjected to a temperature of fifty million degrees centigrade. Our atomic bombs achieve that temperature for a hundred billionths of a second, which is sufficient to ignite the quadium. It should not be too hard to make a quadium bomb, placing the quadium in the center of an atomic bomb. If it is not too hard for us, it should not be too hard for them either. But the atomic bomb, as I said, is the first step. It represents the essential fuse."

The President got up, walked to the window and looked out. "Tell me," he said, with his back to them, "are there any other likely aftereffects of the explosion apart from the appalling destruction caused by the fire and light? Any radiation or other things of that nature?"

"Several rather interesting ones," replied Kokintz slowly. "The neutrons released will, without a doubt, attack the nitrogen in the air, splitting the atomic nuclei and producing a substance known as carbon fourteen. The precise characteristics of carbon fourteen are not understood. But the indications are that it is extremely toxic. There is a strong suggestion that it produces sterility, not only in mammals but also in the soil itself. If that is so, the soil over which this substance drifts and settles would become quite barren. There is also the probability that carbon fourteen may be a factor in the production of monsters, both in the animal kingdom to which, of course, man belongs, and in the vegetable kingdom as well. Carbon fourteen is a remarkably stable substance. It does not readily disintegrate. Once produced by a quadium-bomb explosion, it would drift about the earth for several centuries, destroying all that it touched."

"The aftereffects of the bomb, then, would be much more appalling than the explosion itself?" the President asked.

"Far worse. With a bomb containing the amount of quadium you have before you, the intense heat created would produce enormous windstorms sweeping at hurricane force over whole continents and oceans. These windstorms would be sufficient to produce tidal waves and unprecedented damage over the greater part of the world. No one, of course, could live in the path of such a windstorm. They would be torn apart. Then again, much of the heat of these bombs is concentrated downward to the earth. Volcanic eruptions and earthquakes might follow. It would be like heating a glass globe at one spot. The glass must be expected either to melt, or, if not melt, crack. I do not exaggerate when I say that the effect would be all that could be expected if the sun were to be placed in contact with the earth's surface for the space of, say, a hundred billionths of a second."

"Nothing could survive," Senator Griffin said, more to himself than to the others.

Dr. Kokintz looked sadly at the President. "It has been most interesting work," he said, "though there have been times when I felt the same compassion for you that Mephistopheles had for Faust. When one is engaged alone, as I have been, in a project of this nature, the very mental isolation from one's fellows; the impossibility of imparting one vestige of knowledge to them; the increasing and inevitable sense of a godlike power over the mass of humanity threatens to change the character one builds from childhood." He smiled a little wryly.

THE MOUSE THAT ROARED

"I felt at times," he continued, "that you and all mankind had sold your souls to me for the secret represented by that," and he pointed to the cylinder of quadium. "Even now I am not convinced that all our souls are not forfeit, or at least in jeopardy, as a result of this work. That is what I mean when I talk of Mephistopheles and Faust.

"But, Mr. President, I do not want to be Mephistopheles any more. I want to be a human being again. And as a human being, I want to ask you: do not make this bomb. Do not let it be us, we, the Americans, to whom the Old World has looked for so long, who kill off one quarter or one third of the people on this earth and leave the rest and their children for generations after, to face a fate which we ourselves cannot foretell with any certainty."

It was not the President who replied, but the Secretary of Defense. He spoke in a clipped, metallic voice, quite different from his normal hesitant tone.

"It is not our choice," he said. "The time is running short. Two to five years you estimate. Perhaps less than that. We have got nowhere with attempts at control even of the atom bomb. Whoever has the quadium bomb first has the best chance of survival. This bomb promises world mastery, though of a monstrous kind. The others want mastery, and they prefer a monstrous sort. It is either we who are the masters, or they, and the world, I believe, would prefer it to be us.

"It is not a role we choose, but one which is forced upon us. And every hour counts. They would never agree not to use such a weapon."

"There is no other way? No hope of agreement? No compromise?" Kokintz asked.

"None," said the secretary.

The President picked up the cylinder of quadium and gave it to the scientist, who put it reluctantly in his tobacco pouch.

"Dr. Kokintz," the President said, "I understand that though you have lived the greater part of your life in

America, you were not born in the United States. Do you mind my asking what was your native land?"

"You have probably never heard of it," Kokintz replied, a little surprised. "Indeed, I can scarcely remember it myself. It is a place in the northern foothills of the Alps. A little independent duchy called Grand Fenwick."

6

THE NEWSPAPERS OF MAY 6 THAT YEAR BLAZONED THE
story that sometime in the near future, on a day and at
an hour which was to be kept secret even from the
President, a full-scale air-raid alarm would be enforced
for the whole east coast of the United States. This was
not to be a mere howling of sirens clearing traffic and
people off the streets for ten minutes, and then an all
clear with no one particularly disturbed and half the
population unaware that anything untoward had taken
place.

In view of the development of weapons against
which no complete defense has yet been devised
[the official announcement from the Department of
Defense read] it is necessary to bring home to each
and every member of the public the need for attending to his individual preservation.

The duration of the alert will be for twenty-four
hours or even longer. During that time no one is to
leave whatever place he or she may be in, other than
to go to an air-raid shelter. Those in their homes, far
from any official shelter, must stay there. Air-raid
wardens, with the support of the military establish-
ment, have instructions to see that nobody leaves his
residence, even to search for children who may be
out playing or at school, once the alarm has been
sounded. It will not be permitted to leave homes or
office buildings to obtain food. Restaurants, groceries
and dairies, in common with other businesses, will be
closed down. Extra food should be laid in in advance.

Children in school or out playing will be taken
to shelters and cared for by the Civil Defense
Organization, as will adults in the open at the time
of the alert.

Do not use the telephone. Jamming of lines in case

of a real attack might well cause the loss of hundreds of lives through essential calls not being able to get through.

Do not turn on water faucets. A heavy demand on mains during actual attack could result in firemen being unable to deal with serious fires. Gas must be turned off. Electric current may remain connected so that the public can listen to developments on the radio.

Cars and buses on the streets at the time of the alert are to be abandoned, and the passengers are to go immediately to the nearest air-raid shelter. Subway trains are to take their passengers to the nearest station and disembark them there. The passengers will remain in the station where emergency feeding arrangements have already been established for them.

Ships in east coast harbors, capable of doing so, will proceed immediately to sea. Personnel aboard other ships will evacuate their vessels and go to air-raid shelters.

During the attack, key groups of defense workers, wearing special coverings designed to give them protection from lethal radiation, will undertake special missions. They will visit a number of key buildings in the course of these duties. They are on no account to be impeded or interfered with in any way.

Then followed a long list of things which people might do to provide for the alert, and at the end the admonition: "This is an exercise in preparing for the preservation of yourself, your community, and your nation. It is essential that you do your part."

The warning of the coming alert was broadcast, courtesy of numerous automobile dealers, soap, soup, canned meat, furniture and other manufacturers every fifteen minutes twenty-four hours a day for a week. The same warning was given, at the same intervals and courtesy of much the same sponsors, over television. The Broadway regulars chuckled over the quip of a night-club comedian that, "This disaster comes to you courtesy of the Cosmopolitan Life Insurance Company."

As the days passed, and the warnings continued through every medium of communication—the press, the radio, television, the cinema, from the pulpit and in a host of pronouncements from everyone with the slightest claim to public attention a mild hysteria began to develop and manifest itself in a series of curious reactions.

A rumor, traced to a Brooklyn storekeeper, that salami was the only food acknowledged to be proof against atomic contamination produced such a demand for the sausage that within twenty-four hours there was not a pound of salami to be had in the whole of New York City. A case was reported from the Bronx of a man who had sold his house for two hundred pounds of salami. A food-store proprietor on Staten Island told police that a widow with eight children had offered him her baby for only five pounds of the meat. Eventually, the *New York Times* was compelled to interview half a dozen well-known physicists and obtain from each of them a statement that salami had no special virtues as a food in case of atomic attack. The reporter who obtained the interviews was recommended for a Pulitzer prize.

Hardly had the salami furor died down than another, concerning alcohol, arose. Some one recalled that the United States Navy, in an experiment carried out on mice had made the fascinating discovery that mice, fed enough alcohol to make them paralytic drunk, and then subjected to gamma rays in lethal concentrations, had come through the experience without as much as a hangover. The navy had arrived at two cautious conclusions as a result of the experiment. The first, that mice could hold, by comparison, twice as much alcohol as man without becoming intoxicated. The second that a high percentage of alcohol in the bloodstream of mammals seemed to provide an uncertain but definite degree of immunity from the radiation released by atomic or other nuclear explosions.

The run on bars and liquor stores, when the story gained circulation, exceeded even that which took place following the repeal of prohibition. A form of drunkenness christened "blitz plotz" by a copyreader on the

New York Daily News became acceptable in even the most rigid social circles. Millions took to carrying hip flasks as they had during prohibition. Elderly ladies and high-school students held it prudent to carry a snort of rye, bourbon, Scotch, gin, or vodka in their hand-bags, and "Have a life saver on me" became a familiar and kindly greeting in business circles.

The *Herald Tribune*, jealous of the salami service of the *Times*, undertook to expose the "blitz plotz" fallacy, but ran into unexpected and humiliating difficulties. In the first instance the public, once convinced that it was a patriotic and personally wise precaution to keep a pleasant buzz on all day and night, was loath to be per-suaded otherwise. They liked the idea, and circulation of the *Tribune* commenced to fall off from the opening of the antiblitz-plotz campaign. Then the attempt to obtain forthright statements from scientists to the effect that alcohol provided no protection at all from atomic radiation was only partially successful. The scientists themselves were not convinced that it was not so. The evidence of the mice was irrefutable so far as mice were concerned, they pointed out. While this did not neces-sarily apply to man, the possibility that it did could not be ruled out. A close parallel between mice and men had been demonstrated in a number of other conditions. Not a scientist could be found who would go on record with a flat statement that intoxication provided no im-munity for gamma radiation.

In desperation, the editor of the *Tribune* himself called on Dr. Kokintz in the special laboratory estab-lished for him on the second floor of the administration building of Columbia University, and asked him bluntly, "Dr. Kokintz, would you yourself recommend being drunk during an attack by nuclear weapons?"

Kokintz peered at him through his thick glasses and said, "What else? What else?"

"But," persisted the editor, "are chances of survival greater for the individual if he is intoxicated?"

"With the weapons we have at the present time," Kokintz replied gravely, "neither sobriety nor intoxication will make any difference. There are no chances of survival."

After thinking this statement over, the editor decided to wind up the campaign with a series of statements from the clergy and prominent social workers.

That evening, he dropped in at the St. Regis and had one of their giant martinis in the King Cole Bar. It was, he reflected as he drank it, a completely subconscious reaction—the same kind of unreasoned and primitive urge that drives men to duck their heads when a building falls on them. He decided he would have another while he thought about the matter.

Gradually, but definitely, what had been intended as warning of a mere practice alert, though on an unprecedented scale, evolved, as a result of the mass publicity, the insistent and inescapable repetitions, the emphasis on the omnipotence of the weapon which had inspired the exercise, into a warning of an actual alert in the public mind. The attempts to put down the salami rumor and the alcohol rumor were taken as positive proof that the real thing was to be expected. The belief grew that the United States government had received secret information that a genuine attack with atomic weapons or even worse was to be launched on the east coast. And then, from a mild hysteria, a form of panic developed.

It started with a demand by parents that schools be closed lest, when the alarm was sounded, mothers and fathers be separated from their children. The school authorities, not wishing to be responsible for the care of hosts of children during an alarm of uncertain duration, readily acquiesced in this demand.

Then city workers began to avoid traveling by subway or by bus lest they be caught in these conveyances during the alarm. Three days after the warning of the practice alert was issued subways were carrying less than half their usual quota of commuters. Buses reported their traffic had fallen off sixty per cent. Later, though not much later, wives demanded that their husbands stay at home, and as the conviction grew that a real attack was impending, there was a rush at railway and airline terminals to get out of New York. Businesses closed down, streets and playgrounds were left deserted, and the panic was on.

The full power of all the communication media were again called upon, this time to get over the message that no actual attack was expected. The exercise was to be merely one of preparedness. The international situation was healthy—healthier than it had been at any time since the close of the war. Diplomats attested to this and were supported by generals and admirals. One general, who but ten days previously had advocated an immediate attack upon those nations, which, he said, were intent upon bleeding the United States to death, announced that there was no reason at all why the two sides could not sort out their difference peaceably.

"We are," he said, "on the very verge of peace—a peace which, if cool judgments are allowed to prevail, must last through our lifetimes and those of our children."

All this, however—the unwavering insistence that this was to be but a practice in preparedness, the unqualified statements of diplomats, generals, and admirals that no war was in sight, even a press conference in which the President assured the nation that there was no danger of attack by any foreign nation or combination of foreign nations—all this had little effect. One question remained unanswered in the public mind: Why have such a large-scale practice if there is no possibility of war breaking out immediately?

Then the one thing happened which, even if the attempt to allay the panic had made any headway, would have canceled all the progress achieved.

Senator Griffin, seriously disturbed by a thousand letters a day from people all over the country, demanding to know whether the United States had any adequate weapons with which to defend itself, decided to announce that the quadium bomb had been perfected. He did so only after consulting with the President, the

Secretary of Defense, and other members of the cabinet. He urged on them that the only way to allay the panic was to assure the public that the United States was in possession of such tremendous destructive capacity that no other nation would dare to attack it.

As chairman of the Atomic Energy Commission, he called a press conference and gave the details of the bomb to the reporters who crowded into the Senate committee room.

"The Q-bomb, which has been perfected by Dr. Kokintz," he said, "gives us the ability, as it were, to summon the flaming sun down upon our enemies. It will, in its present size, devastate an area of two million square miles. There is no limit to the power of destruction which is now in our hands.

"Needless to say," he added, "we will never use the Q-bomb unless we are compelled to do so."

"What would compel us to use it?" a reporter asked.

"I can conceive of no circumstance other than its use first by some other nation," the Senator replied. And immediately he realized he was guilty of a gross error.

"Does that mean that other nations have the Q-bomb?" the reporter asked.

"Not to our knowledge," the Senator parried, and he had hardly uttered the reply than he realized that he had now sown the suspicion that other nations might have this weapon. He hurriedly closed the press conference before any more damage was done. He did so with the reiteration that with the Q-bomb in its possession, no one would dare attack the United States. But he was uncomfortably conscious that the point had not gone over and the press conference had been a failure. His suspicions proved correct.

In the midst of the reports, printed over the nation's front pages, that the United States was the possessor of the frightful weapon was the hint that others either had the same weapon or were likely to develop it shortly. And hardly had this news been absorbed by the public, than the great alert was sounded.

It commenced at six in the morning of May 13 with a

wail from a thousand sirens in New York, Philadelphia,
Boston and Washington. The wail rose to such a cre-
scendo that it seemed all the potentialities of mere
sound had been exhausted and some new kind of sen-
sation, a combination of sound, pain and physical pressure, had been developed. Then the sirens slipped
dolefully from their peak down and down and then up
again and then down again. And when they were quiet,
they left behind such a silence that it seemed as if there
were not in the whole of America as much noise as
would be caused by the snapping of a twig. It was as if
the sirens themselves had slain all living matter.

In every part of the east coast, those in the streets, at
the first moan of the alert, had stood paralyzed by
fright, and then flung themselves into doorways and
into houses, down cellar steps and into subways and
air-raid shelters; some sobbing, some laughing, some
with their breath coming in hard little gasps, and others
quite incapable of breathing for the while.

On the New York waterfront, there was a scurrying
from ships as longshoremen, stevedores, and crews deserted vessels which had no steam up, and scampered
to safety. One ship alone cleared the docks and that
under her own power. The R.M.S. *Queen Mary* swung
slowly out to midstream, turned around and headed
down the Hudson, the captain on the bridge himself
giving orders to the quartermaster, who stood at the
wheel beside him. When they cleared the river, he
called for full-speed ahead and an hour later, well out
to sea, sighted a small brig headed toward the Hudson.

The captain, after describing the time of the air-raid
alarm and the sailing of his vessel, made the following
notation in his log:

> Sighted 300-ton brig *Endeavor* ten miles off
> Ambrose light. Called her on loud hailer and told
> her to put about as vessels were forbidden to enter
> Port of New York. No reply to first message. On re-
> peating warning second time was met with flight of
> arrows from brig. Vessel undamaged. Continued on
> course.

7

THE BRIG *Endeavor*, THE DOUBLE-HEADED EAGLE BANNER of the duchy of Grand Fenwick broken out at her main peak, swept up the deserted Hudson before a brisk easterly. Tully Bascomb and the captain were the only men aboard who knew precisely where they were and both were puzzled that they had not, since firing upon the *Queen Mary* and hoistering their colors, sighted as much as a tug or a coast-guard cutter. It was a dancing May morning, the sun sparkling on the greenish water, glanced off the skyscrapers that stood like the spears of a vast host gathered on the island of Manhattan. The air was so clear that Tully felt it might be drunk as well as breathed. And yet over all there lay an appalling and ghostly silence, as though this were not a real city but only a painting of one, done upon a vast canvas and representing some metropolis, deserted by its inhabitants centuries before.

"This is New York," Tully said to Will Tatum, his lieutenant. "But I don't understand why there is not an enemy in sight. We have the whole river and harbor to ourselves. Usually it is as thick with craft as a flypaper with flies."

"They have realized at last that we were in earnest," said Will glumly, "and have probably set an ambush for us. We must go carefully. Those buildings are the biggest I've ever seen and will take a lot of storming. I wonder why the Americans build such big castles. I had not heard that they were often attacked."

Will, a man built on the proportions of an ox, was noted rather for his physical than mental strength. He pulled a one hundred and twenty pound bow, stood six feet three inches and had never been out of Grand Fenwick in his life. A man of more imagination would have been awed by the size of the city that lay before him to be taken. Indeed, the rest of the expeditionary force, lined along the bulwarks of the *Endeavor,* were looking at the Manhattan skyline in grim and desperate silence. But Will saw in the task merely a job which was to be done, in which blows would be given and taken, but which, nonetheless, would be successfully completed in the end.

The expeditionary force, which on the voyage over had worn civilian dress, was now uniformed in all the equipage of war. The twenty bowmen had their pot helmets upon their heads. Their hauberks of chain mail, worn over leather shirts, covered neck, chest, and back. Each had six bowstrings of deer sinew tied around his waist and each a small shield on his left arm, a short sword slung beside it, and a longbow across his back. Tully looked them over, and told himself that they would do well for him and their nation. The three men at arms—Will being among them—wore white surcoats over their armor, blazoned with the eagle crest. They carried besides longbows, maces with wicked spiked heads.

"Pedro—" Tully called to the captain of the brig, who had come to the conclusion since the chartering of his vessel in Marseilles that this was all something connected with the movies and maybe he ought to treble the price— "Pedro, bring me into the Cunard dock at the bottom of Forty-fourth Street. We will make our assault there."

"They'll make the devil of a fuss if I do," said Pedro. "The first thing you know, there'll be customs officials, harbormaster's men, policemen, and shipping clerks all waving me away and they'll probably levy a fine more than the brig is worth. I don't know why nobody has come to give me permission to dock. The health department should have met us off the harbor. Maybe they all had a big week end and they're sleeping late. It's Monday morning."

"This," said Tully, "is war."

"Okay. It's war," said Pedro, like someone humoring a child. "But I don't see any cameramen about to take publicity shots. Maybe we ought to hang around a bit until they turn up."

"Dock," roared Tully. "Dock before I have off your ears."

"Aye. Aye," said Pedro. "Stand by the main braces there." His crew of five scrambled aft, Pedro put his helm over, the main yards swung round until the sails were backed and the *Endeavor* slipped prettily under her own way into the Cunard dock where the crew made her fast fore and aft to bollards.

"Men of Grand Fenwick," cried Tully as soon as the ship was secured. "I have led you to the heartland of the enemy. Follow to victory." He threw a rope with a grappling hook at the end of it onto the dock overhead. Three other ropes followed and the men swarmed up them to form ranks on the quay.

"Hey," called Pedro from down below. "What about me? What do you want me to do?"

"Stand by to make sail on our return," said Tully.

"Do you expect to be long?"

Tully looked up the street and around at the vast but deserted city that seemed to be waiting for him and his little army like some trap of steel and concrete which at any moment would be sprung to destroy them.

"I cannot say," he said. And then to his men, "Banners advance in the cause of Grand Fenwick."

Now that he was in New York City, Tully had no very clear idea of what to do next, though he was careful to hide his lack of plan from his men. He had intended a landing on the coast with his force in civilian clothing, then marching upon Washington, or perhaps taking a train, and storming the White House. A quick and determined blow, struck with surprise, he felt would give him as a hostage for terms of peace, the President of the United States himself. But the plan had met with surprising opposition from among his own lieutenants, and Will Tatum, who before their departure had had a private interview with Gloriana, would not be moved to agree with it.

"We must wage honorable war," Will had said, "under arms and meeting the enemy in the open. If we fight by guile we will be more footpads than soldiers."

Tully, thinking the thing over, had had to agree, and since it was he who in the first instance had insisted upon honor in the matter, was a little ashamed of having deviated from his principles. The trouble was that here he was in New York with his army, but there wasn't anyone to fight. He had expected to have to exchange some hard knocks even to gain a landing. He had expected that they might be set upon at sea, which was the reason he had ordered the volley of arrows loosed at the *Queen Mary.* But there was not as much as a corporal's guard to oppose him. He decided to march down Forty-fourth Street to Times Square in the hope of meeting the enemy.

The deserted street, the mute buildings, the silent air, the empty doorways, the corners and ledges and chinks and buttresses of the city resounded strangely to the sound of the marching of the army of Grand Fenwick as it strode towards the center of New York City. It was a sound never before heard in the New World— a sound so strange to the Old that the very leaves of the forest would have turned to listen to it—the sound of mailed feet clinking upon the road. The lone banner of the double-headed eagle fluttered in the breeze, the white surcoats of the men at arms made brave splashes in the sunlight, the helmets of the bowmen gleamed, but only the birds witnessed the pageant.

One or two of the men coughed in the silence and then feeling that this cough had been heard for at least a mile, eyed each other uneasily. A cat came from around a corner, mewed loudly and fled. Those who saw it laughed nervously; those who didn't but heard only the mewing started. A flock of pigeons wheeled suddenly down upon the band out of the sunlight, and only the iron discipline of their training prevented the men from breaking ranks. A sheet of newspaper, caught by a gust of wind, followed them up the street like some mischievous urchin, now coming abreast of the

marching ranks, now dropping mockingly behind only to
dart ahead again. Eventually it wrapped itself around
Tully's legs and would not be shaken off, making him
feel ridiculous. He stooped and picked it up and thrust
it into his sword belt angrily. But beyond these little
noises and movements, normally lost in the city's roar,
there was no sound or stirring other than that which they
themselves made.

So they went, still without meeting a soul, until they
had arrived at Times Square. The Old *New York
Times* building stood alone and quite deserted in the
empty crossroads of the world, and catching sight of it,
Tully decided that it should be taken. It would provide
in the first instance a temporary fortress. Its capture, he
hoped, would get the war started on some more tangible
basis. And it would be a good place to hold a council
of war and seek for some reason why while New York
was where it had always been, none of the New Yorkers
were.

On the ground floor was a drugstore, whose windows,
bright with a thousand attractive geegaws, fascinated the
men of Grand Fenwick.

"Will," said Tully to his lieutenant, "take half the men
over to the other side of the building. You will find a
door there. When I cry 'Charge' break it down and kill
any who offer resistance. We will breach the door on this
side at the same moment."

Will saluted and trooped off with his men, who, despite their discipline, could not resist dawdling as they
passed the drugstore windows with their display of mechanical pencils and pens, wallets, handbags, cigarettes,
pipes, and cigarette lighters. In the center was a big sign
which said, STOCK MUST BE MOVED. "Come on,"
said Will to his lagging warriors, "we will attend to that
later."

On the other side they found a brass double door and
gathered around to burst this open at the word of command from Tully. When it came, six muscular shoulders
crashed into the doors, which, since they were not locked,
spilled the company into the lobby of the building. At

the same moment the remainder of the force under Tully's command charged the door on their side. This also was unsecured, so they tumbled into the drugstore, and plunging through, piled into their comrades in the lobby.

A few blows were exchanged and a sword or two brought ringing down upon helmets before it was discovered that the lobby of the building was deserted except for themselves. Again there was an anticlimax. Again what had been anticipated would prove a dour assault at arms had turned out to be an unnecessarily forceful entry. Again, all had been prepared to meet the enemy face to face only to be confronted by a complete absence of the enemy. The men stood in little clumps, bewildered, looking nervously around and muttering to each other.

"Will," said Tully, drawing his lieutenant aside, "to be plain about it, I don't like this at all. I don't understand why there is nobody in the city."

"You don't think it is because they knew we were coming?" asked Will, who was beginning to doubt such a reason himself.

"No. I don't. It's more like as if there had been a plague."

Will blanched. He was a brave man; none braver. But he had a mortal fear of germs, which it had been explained to him in his youth would certainly devour him if he did not wash behind his ears. "The air smells bad here," he said.

"It always does," replied Tully.

"You don't suppose these blobs of black stuff on the ground are some kind of germ warfare, do you?"

"No. Well, in a way they are. They're old pieces of chewing gum, tons of it. Probably filthy with microbes, but they never bothered New Yorkers before. We've got to find someone to let them know that they've been invaded. We've got to strike a blow somewhere. An invasion doesn't count if nobody ever finds out about it."

He put his hand on his sword belt in deep thought, and in doing so, rediscovered the sheet of newspaper which had caught on his legs as he marched up Forty-fourth Street. He was about to hurl it from him when he decided, on a hunch, to look it over and see whether there might be any clue in it to the reason for the desertion of the city.

The sheet turned out to be the front page of the *New York Times* of the day before. A double banner, eight columns wide, spread underneath the masthead. One line read: SUPERBOMB ANNOUNCED BY GRIFFIN. The other: EAST COAST ALERT EXPECTED HOURLY. There was a morass of other headings and then the text of the two stories. "The United States is in possession of an ultimate weapon of mass destruction capable of devastating an area of two million square miles," the first story read, and went on to describe how this had been announced by Senator Griffin of the Atomic Energy Commission, and that the bomb had been developed by Dr. Kokintz of Columbia University. The second story, which ran side by side with the first, said that it was learned from usually well-informed sources that the alert of the whole east coast of the United States, in preparation for atomic attack, was likely to be held within the next twenty-four hours.

Tully read both stories through twice before the significance of the situation dawned on him. He reduced it to two basic points. The first was that New York was likely to be atom bombed within a matter of hours, maybe minutes. The second, was that a far more valuable man to seize than the President of the United States was Dr. Kokintz of Columbia University. And Dr. Kokintz had better be seized quickly before whatever other enemy the United States was at war with blew up New York and won the issue before Grand Fenwick had a chance.

"Form up the men and get them out into the street," he shouted to Will with sudden decision. "We haven't much time to win this war and have to march about eight miles."

"Where are we going?" Will asked.

"Columbia University," Tully replied.

8

THE INVASION OF THE UNITED STATES BY THE EXPEDITION-
ary force of the duchy of Grand Fenwick was under
way nearly two hours before anyone in an official position,
or indeed in any position at all, realized that such a thing
was taking place. Even when the presence of strange
armed men in Manhattan was discovered, no one had any
immediate conception of the significance of the matter.

The elaborate plans made to guard the civilian population by keeping them off the street, irrespective of what
excuses or devices they might invent, were fully successful. The first shock of the long-awaited air-raid warning
had been sufficient to send all scurrying to places of safety. But the Secretary of Defense realized that this initial
shock would be replaced in a little while by a growing
curiosity as to what was going on. And this curiosity, he
reasoned, would be most marked in New York and its
environs.

Thus air-raid wardens had been told to stay in shelters
in subway terminals and in buildings, and prevent anyone leaving. In this task they were helped by the police,
who also remained below ground. Other defense workers, decontamination men, unexploded bomb experts,
medical and ambulance corps and volunteers with food
were to appear in the streets as soon as practicable after
the alert to make sure that all was as well as could be
expected. Starting from a number of key points around
the city, they were to inspect every building and shelter,
take care of pregnant women, infants, the infirm and the
aged and see that all were supplied with food, water, and
clothing. But no others were to be allowed on the surface. Thus it was not until an hour and a half after their
assault upon the deserted city that the men of Grand
Fenwick met with the first of their enemies.

They had, by that time, marching up Broadway under Tully's leadership, gone as far as One Hundredth Street without seeing a soul or being seen.

Then at the intersection of One Hundredth and Broadway, they came, quite unexpectedly, upon a party of five men, dressed as no other men Tully had ever seen. They wore cumbersome gray-white suits, which covered them from head to foot, with thick glass windows in the cowls through which they could see. They were huddled together, and carried small instruments which they held to the sides of buildings, against fire hydrants and close to the ground while peering at them anxiously. The two parties saw each other in the same moment, and were equally horrified at each other's appearance. Both suspected that they were in the presence of an invasion force of monsters from another world. Both halted, and the decontamination squad, for such they were, began edging away, while the bowmen fitted arrows to the strings of their bows.

One of the Americans, his voice humming and burbling through his cumbersome suit and further distorted by panic, cried, "They're off a flying saucer." The words were no sooner spoken than they took the force of divine revelation, confirming a suspicion forming but up to then uncrystallized in the minds of the others.

"Flying saucer," cried another, and in a twinkling the whole party had turned and scampered around the corner, heading for the river. Finding themselves severely handicapped in flight by their suits, the decontamination men tore them off and flung them away. In a second the quiet streets were reverberating to cries of "Flying Saucer! Men from Mars! Ray guns!" and the panic was increased by a volley of arrows which whistled over the heads of the fleeing five and went clashing and chattering along the roads and buildings.

A second volley was about to follow the first, but Tully, concerned over the prospect of an atom bomb falling at any minute upon New York, ordered his men to cease fire and continue their marching toward Columbia University. As an afterthought he picked up the discarded suits, and gave them to some of the Fenwickians to carry.

The leader of the decontamination squad, a man of middle years who had not missed a newspaper comic section as far back as he could remember, was the first to recover his presence of mind. He had run himself almost out of breath when he became conscious that he had a duty other than flight to perform. And that duty, he knew, consisted of reporting to headquarters that a detachment of invaders from a flying saucer, perhaps from several flying saucers, had landed in New York, were marching through the city in metal clothing, were equipped with ray guns that threw a kind of dart that whistled as it went, and thousands more were probably to be expected at any minute.

He realized, as his first terror left him, that he might have some difficulty in getting anyone to believe his story, though there was no doubt in his own mind that the horde of men who had stolen up on him and his party were not human and must therefore be from another planet. For one thing, they appeared taller than most human beings, a good foot or more. Then their heads had no hair on them but seemed to be made of metal. Furthermore they glittered in the sunlight. And lastly they had launched some sort of supersonic hand missile which made a whistling noise as it sped over his head.

All this he straightened out in his mind as he phoned the secret number to which reports were to be turned in, from a corner telephone booth.

"Give me Special Reports," he said when his call was answered.

There was a short silence and a voice said, "Special Reports. What is your name and section?"

"Tom Mulligan. Section 4-300, subsection 3. Decontamination," he replied.

There was the noise of a paper being put into a typewriter and then the clicking of the keys as this information was typed out. "Okay. Go ahead," Special Reports said.

"There's a bunch of men from a flying saucer at Broadway and One Hundredth," Tom said breathlessly.

"How many?" came back the laconic reply.

"Maybe fifty or sixty of them," replied Tom, relieved that he was apparently being believed.

"Just a minute, while I type this out. Fifty or sixty men from a flying saucer—say, what the hell is this? What do you mean, flying saucer?"

"Just what I said," replied Tom. "I saw them. My squad saw them. Fifty or sixty. With metal heads, and all covered in some kind of shiny stuff. They appeared suddenly right in front of us, and fired on us with some kind of a ray gun."

"Listen, bub," said Special Reports, "you have been told to keep out of saloons, haven't you? The job you're doing is a serious business. You're not supposed to get your nose wet. Where are you now?"

"Ninety-eighth and Broadway," said Tom. "And I haven't been in any saloons. Ask my men. They were with me. They saw these guys. Right out of a flying saucer. I tell you the city is being invaded."

"Stay where you are," said Special Reports. "I'll send someone over." But before the Civil Defense official arrived to pick Tom up for questioning, another patrol appeared. They had already picked up his men, dressed in ordinary clothing and jabbering about flying saucers. None had any identification. To humor them, since all told substantially the same story, the patrol drove them all to the place where they said they had left their decontamination suits. Not finding them there, they hustled them off to the nearest subway shelter where they were thrust into the depths without ceremony. Here Tom and his men tried hard to convince the wardens on duty that they were part of the Civil Defense Organization and had been interrupted in the course of their duties by a war party—which had now grown to half a division— from Mars.

"Blitz plotz," the wardens said understandingly.

The word of an invasion from Mars, however, with frightful details of giant beings in metal suits, men

equipped with strange and awesome weapons, spread
from mouth to mouth among the teeming, scared, credu-
lous multitude in the subway station. Their nerves had
been keyed up for a full week. They had been warned
of weapons which defeated all attempts of the imagination to describe. They had read innumerable stories of
flying saucers; they had devoured a host of books on adventures in space; they had seen movies depicting every
kind of invader from every kind of other world. They
had been huddled underground and kept there, and they
swallowed the story of an invasion from Mars, readily,
avidly, and almost with relief. At last they knew who
the enemy was whose onslaught they had been preparing
to meet for seven days.

"Men from Mars," the cry went and it spread from
the Ninety-sixth Street subway station to the Seventy-
second, and on down the line until, in a comparatively
short while, all who had been caught in the subways of
New York at the sounding of the air-raid alarm were telling each other that the city had been taken over by an
expeditionary force from a neighboring planet.

The reactions were curious. Some wanted to get out
and have a look and had to be forcibly restrained. Others
crept out of the subway stations down the tunnels, anxious to escape even further into the ground. Somebody
started singing "Abide with Me" in a high-pitched qua-
ver, and the hymn was taken up tentatively at first and
then with more vigor, so that soon the chant was echoing
through the underground passages, the echoes seeming
louder than the voices which roused them.

From below the streets the voices emerged booming
but still recognizable from manholes and gratings into
the empty city. The wardens and police started to worry.
Several called up Special Reports to say that they didn't
know how long they could control the people in the subways. "Abide with Me" gave way to "Mairzy Doats" then
to "The Little Doggie in the Window" and, in the brief
intervals, the tales grew wilder until it was common
knowledge that flying saucers had landed on top of all

the principal buildings in Manhattan, unleashing hordes of steel men who flung electric rays from their hands.

Special Reports at first told the wardens to do what they could to control the crowds and that reinforcements would be sent. But as the reinforcements went out only to send back messages that the situation was getting completely out of hand, it was decided to call up the Secretary of Defense. The decision was not an easy one to make, for the strictest instructions had been given to New York Civil Defense Headquarters that the secretary was to be contacted only in case of a pressing emergency.

Did half a million people in the New York subway system singing "The Little Doggie in the Window" constitute a pressing emergency? General Snippett, Civil Defense Chief for the New York area, asked himself. He was not sure that it did. He was a practical man who had achieved the rank of general in the course of his army career largely by refusing to be panicked by anything. People singing didn't constitute in itself an emergency, in his definition of the term, though he abominated music. So in the first instance he had temporized by sending out even more reinforcements, and sound trucks calling upon those in subways and shelters to keep calm and assuring them that nothing untoward had happened.

The sound trucks, unfortunately, produced the exact opposite effect to that desired on those in the underground tunnels. They sounded like giants shouting in the streets, and their message "There are no men from Mars around" did not get over in its entirety. Some heard it correctly, but most caught only the phrase "Men from Mars around." Two of the trucks, rounding a corner from opposite directions, the drivers distracted by the singing coming from underground, collided, and the gasoline tank on one exploded with a soft "whoomp." This gave rise to a new rumor to the effect that an atomic bomb had been dropped. Some in the subways insisted that they had radiation sickness. Others shouted that the heat was increasing and perhaps half the city was already burning. The clamor of fire engines racing to the blazing trucks lent credence to this last rumor; and it was at this point, with distracted wardens jamming the Special Reports section with appeals for aid, that General Snippett decided to call the Secretary of Defense.

"Mr. Secretary," he said, when he had obtained his connection on a direct line to Washington, "I have to report an emergency situation in New York. There are half a million people in the subways. They are all of them singing some kind of tommyrot. And most of them believe that the city has been invaded by men from Mars. The defense workers, special and regular police and every man I have available are trying to keep them underground. But I don't know how much longer we can restrain them."

There was a short silence on the line and General Snippett was conscious that he had reached a crisis in his career. If he could not convince the secretary that this nonsense was not of his own doing, he could look forward to spending the remainder of his life in enforced idleness, living on a pension inadequate to his standards of living. The secretary's first question was not reassuring.

"Did you say men from Mars?" he asked crisply.

"Yes, sir," replied the general. Again there was a short silence.

"How did this nonsense get started?"

"I've traced it to a phone call to our own Special Reports section. A Civil Defense squad leader by the name of Mulligan turned in a report that a group of men from Mars had landed in a flying saucer as part of an invasion force. They threw some kind of a dart at him and his squad. They were dressed in metal coverings."

"Was he drunk?" the secretary asked.

"That was our belief. He was told to remain where he was while a patrol went out to bring him in. But when the patrol arrived he had—ahem—disappeared."

"Disappeared?"

"Yes. There was no trace of him."

"No trace at all?"

"None."

"What about his men?"

"They had disappeared also."

"No trace?"

"No trace."

Another silence.

"Tell me, General," the secretary asked dryly, "as an army man, do you place any credence in the navy report that alcohol is an antidote for atomic radiation?"

"None whatever," replied the general fervently.

"I am relieved to hear that. Now, have you seen any of these men from Mars yourself?"

"No."

"Flying saucers or anything like that?"

"No."

"Well, will you kindly go out and make a personal inspection of the city from the Battery to the Bronx, and return and report to me. In the meantime, do whatever is possible to stop this tomfoolery in the subways. This sort of nonsense can ruin an exercise designed to protect the largest city of our nation—a city I need hardly stress that has been entrusted to your care. You might ponder, while on your tour, over the fact that no reports have been received from Boston of men from Mars or flying saucers. I hardly think that invaders from another world would be so well informed of local temperament and excitability in the United States as to select New York over Boston as a place to start operations. Report to me in an hour."

There was the firm cold click of a receiver being placed back on its hook and General Snippett contemplated the telephone in his hand for a stunned and wrathful moment.

"Tasker!" he roared to his aide. "Get my car!"

9

DR. KOKINTZ, SECLUDED IN HIS SOUNDPROOF LABORATORY
on the second floor of the administration building of Columbia University, had not been paying much attention
to the air-raid preparations. He was a bachelor and this
gave him all the freedom of place and time he felt his
work required. He had contrived living quarters of a
kind for himself in the laboratory, and convinced his
landlady that when he did not return home for a day
or two—he roomed in an ample boardinghouse of the
McKinley era in Brooklyn—it was not because he was
drunk, nor had he been knocked down by a car, nor had
he been out with a girl friend. He had either fallen
asleep in a movie, gone to Washington, or was busy
working.

Mrs. Reiner, his landlady, a woman of motherly proportions and temperament, never quite believed this. But
she did not question him about his habits, though his
occasional overnight absences disturbed her greatly. It
was not right for bachelors to remain out overnight, to
her way of thinking. It was ridiculous when they did so,
that they should expect anyone to believe that they were
working. And it was even more ridiculous to say that
they were working in Columbia University. The only
people who worked in Columbia University at nighttime,
to her knowledge, were janitors, and Dr. Kokintz was
not a janitor. There was, Mrs. Reiner knew, something
peculiar about Dr. Kokintz, but he paid his rent regularly, and liked his birds. And Mrs. Reiner liked birds too
and undertook to feed the doctor's for him when he was
away. He in return gave her his private telephone number in the university, so she could call him up if he were
away for any great length of time, but he asked her not
to call him at night. Thus it was that Mrs. Reiner of

Acacia Street, Brooklyn, and the President of the United States were the only two people in all America who could call Dr. Kokintz on his private line in his secret nuclear physics laboratory. All others had to make their calls through the university switchboard.

It was not disinterest in the air-raid preparations that caused Dr. Kokintz's indifference to them. Rather, it was precisely because of the preparations that he had been so preoccupied. For Dr. Kokintz was busy perfecting the quadium bomb whose imminence as a practical weapon had inspired the great practice alert.

Senator Griffin had stated, it is true, in a vain attempt to reassure the public, that the United States already possessed the Q-bomb. That was not an incorrect statement. The bomb he referred to, however, was an extremely clumsy contrivance which Dr. Kokintz had put together at the behest of the President and the Secretary of Defense and which he had dismantled immediately because he wasn't satisfied with it.

What he wanted to get was a small bomb, a neat package of a bomb which could be carried by any kind of aircraft anywhere. What he had put together for the President was something as big and as clumsy as a packing case. His professional training, calling for the most scrupulous tidiness and nicety, was offended by it, and demanded something immeasurably neater. The work was intensely interesting to him as a perfectionist. The ultimate result of the work—the widespread devastation which it could cause, the frightful carbon fourteen which it might release to roll like the very breath of death over vast areas, sterilizing the air and ground—horrified him as a human being. But the perfectionist in him had received more training than the human being, and so he had continued with the task.

He had finished now. On the work bench before him was a small, gray, lead container, the size and shape of a shoebox. This was the world's only quadium bomb. It looked quite harmless, but the charge was so delicately triggered—he had used as a spring, part of a hairpin obtained from Mrs. Reiner, his landlady—that a heavy knock or jar would be sufficient to explode it. Dr. Kokintz had not yet devised the safety devices which would prevent the accidental setting off of his Q-bomb. That was a comparatively simple matter which he could attend to in a little while. The bomb came first and the bomb was finished.

"Dickey," he said to the canary in a nearby cage, his sole companion in the laboratory, "let us both be very careful indeed. It is time for us to eat, and I will let you out for a while to fly around. But promise me that you won't knock that box on the floor because if you do it will vaporize you and everybody in New York City. Myself included."

The canary chirruped a bright peal of melody.

"I know you are too small to knock the box down," Dr. Kokintz continued. "It is just that I am nervous. I really ought to take it apart, but I am tired and my hands are trembling. So we will leave it until we have eaten something and then we will take it apart and then go home to sleep."

He reached into his pocket for his sandwich, found first his pipe and his tobacco as he almost always did, put them absent-mindedly on the bench and searched some more. He found a wax-paper package which he pulled out and opened dubiously, discovering two pieces of brown bread in which lay two slices of liver sausage. He peered at them through his thick glasses. They looked as though they had once had life but had died between the slices of bread. In the other pocket was another package, but the sandwich it contained was even more suspicious in appearance.

"Dickey," the scientist said, "I have had these sandwiches two days, perhaps three, and I don't think we should eat them. I'll call the girl on the switchboard and see whether she will send out for some for me." He picked up the telephone and dialed "O," which would give him the university switchboard. But after two or three minutes there was no reply.

"Strange," he said, looking at his watch, "it is only 10:30. Surely she cannot have gone to lunch yet." He dialed once again, this time waiting longer and eventually a voice answered. It surprised him that it was a man's voice for he could never recall the switchboard being run by a man.

"What is it?" the voice said in such a way as to convey that whatever it was, it was certainly not worth interrupting the speaker for.

"It is Dr. Kokintz," the physicist said, "I wanted to get the girl to see whether she could get me a sandwich."

"Dr. Kokintz?" said the voice, immediately solicitous. "This is the building warden. Where are you?"

"In my laboratory. Who did you say you were?"

"The air-raid warden for the building. There's an air-raid alert on, you know."

"An air-raid alert? Are we at war so soon? Nobody said anything to me about it. I think I ought to have been told."

The voice laughed reassuringly. "No. There's no war, Doctor. That's just a lot of talk. We wardens know there's no war. But this is a real big warning. You can't leave the building. As a matter of fact, you'd better stay where you are until someone comes up to take you down to the shelter."

"But I can't go down to the shelter. I've got something here that I dare not leave. It is imperative that I do not leave it."

"Oh . . . it's not your canary, is it? I think we can take care of that."

"No, it's not my canary. It's something much different. I can't leave it and I'm hungry. Can't someone get me a sandwich?"

The air-raid warden thought hard for a minute. Then he recalled that emergency canteen workers would be around soon with food for those caught by the air-raid sirens without any.

"Just stay where you are a minute, will you, Doc?" he said. "There'll be someone up with food in a minute or two. But promise me you won't leave."

"I promise the whole of New York City that I will not leave," the doctor replied gravely.

The warden laughed, hung up, and went to see if there was any sign of the canteen workers coming.

In the meantime Tully and his men, marching fast, reached the university to find it as devoid of life, as menacingly silent, as dead as all the other buildings which they had passed in the tomblike city. Tully was becoming increasingly anxious and tense. With each minute that went by, he was sure his prospects of seizing the one prize which would bring the United States to its knees were dimming. It was for him, and the expeditionary force of Grand Fenwick, a race against time. If they could capture this Dr. Kokintz and his bomb before the city was attacked, and get him back on board the brig and set sail, victory would be theirs. But if the city were atom bombed first, then he and all his men would certainly be killed and the whole venture would come to nothing.

Oddly he was not particularly afraid of dying. It was the thought of failing Gloriana, his duchess, that disturbed him. He tried to convince himself that this was a matter of patriotism, that it was love of his country that made him so anxious and so determined to win a resounding victory. But he had to admit secretly that it was more than that. It was Gloriana with the golden hair, the soft persuasive voice, the smile that was as gentle and as personal as a blessing. For the men the war was perhaps one of patriotism. But for himself, though it had started that way, it was rapidly becoming a matter of knight errantry.

The party skirted the university buildings to find all the doors securely bolted, all windows and gates shut, and no means of entry, short of force, available. Tully decided to break in at the main entrance of the administration block.

"Will," he said to his lieutenant, "cut down that tree, make a battering ram of it, and force the main door."

Cutting down the tree, a small linden growing out of the sidewalk, was no easy matter. In common with all New York trees, it had to be protected from the people for whose pleasure it had been planted. So there was a stout iron fencing around it, which needed to be battered apart with maces. The noise of the heavy clubs, ringing on the iron, echoed strangely through the quiet streets, disturbing the pigeons which went fluttering away. But the blows served to steady the nerves of the men, for the quiet had affected them all, with the exception of Will who still secretly believed that the city had been evacuated at the news of the outbreak of war with Grand Fenwick.

Once the fencing had been beaten down, it was a simple task to fell the tree, strip it of its branches, and turn it into a pole suitable for use as a battering ram. Will, who was particularly skillful at this kind of work, reinforced the head of the ram by wrapping a coat of mail around it, securing this in place with leather straps.

"A breach for Grand Fenwick," he roared. "Remember our Pinot."

The ram was seized by eight of the bowmen who raced up a flight of shallow stone steps with it, to hurl it crashing against the door. A boom like the beating of an enormous drum resulted. The door shook and seemed to cough, as it were, from the blow which it had received in its stomach. But it held firm.

"Again," cried Will. "Twice more and we are in."

As it was, it took but once more. The university door, strong enough to withstand the high spirits of twentieth-century students, was yet not able to hold fast against the breaching tactics of fourteenth-century warriors. It seemed to shrug its hinges in helpless acquiescence and then flung open, the men of Fenwick stumbling inside with their ram. They found themselves in a large hall, again quite empty, quite silent and quite devoid of a trace of the foe.

"The devil," cried Will. "I'd like nothing better than that they'd come out and fight. It's a hard job for twenty men to search a city this size for a smell of the enemy. If we had but one good battle and they officially surrendered, we could send them all about their business and get something to eat."

"We are nearer to victory than you think, but our time

is running short," Tully replied. He was standing before a large directory on the wall, scanning it for a particular name. "Ah, there it is," he said, half to himself. "Dr. Kokintz. Room 201. That will be on the second floor. Leave the men on guard here and outside, and follow me upstairs. If anyone approaches, they are to be either taken or killed."

Tully raced up the stairs, two at a time, his broadsword drawn and Will behind him. On the left-hand side of a corridor at the head of the flight, he found a door marked Room 201. It was shut, but with one hard jab of his foot, near the lock, he flung it open. Dr. Kokintz, surrounded by a welter of retorts and scales and test tubes and glass condensers, stood in the center of his laboratory, blinking at them. He took off his glasses, rubbing them briefly on a corner of his jacket and put them on again.

"Did you bring my sandwiches?" he asked.

10

FEW IN THE HISTORY OF HUMAN WARFARE HAVE BEEN SO
difficult to convince that they had been taken prisoner
by an enemy as was Dr. Kokintz when captured by Tully
Bascomb in the name of Grand Fenwick. He had, it is
true, good reason for his disbelief. For one thing, he had
been expecting sandwiches and he had got, instead,
broadswords. For another, he had anticipated that a
twentieth-century air-raid warden would be up to see
him with coffee and comfort. Instead he was confronted
by two fourteenth-century men at arms, clad in chain
mail, and covered from shoulders to calves with surcoats
on which were emblazed a double-headed eagle, ram-
pant. Finally, in common with the whole United States,
he had no idea that the nation had been invaded, and
invaded by the duchy of Grand Fenwick.

Even for a man who kept in touch with current events,
the situation would have been astonishing. For Dr. Kokintz, who as a scientist was more familiar with the future and the past than the present, it was beyond immediate comprehension.

"No sandwiches," he said for the third time, blinking at
Tully as if he had risen through the floor boards and
was likely to disappear by the same route at any minute.
Tully told him for the third time, with creditable patience, that there were no sandwiches and that he was
a prisoner of war.

"I do not understand it," the doctor said, shaking his
head from side to side quite slowly. "I do not understand
it. I believe I must have been working too hard and am
suffering from hallucinations. You two"—pointing to
them—"are a hallucination. You are the result of my
working too hard. The mind, when overpressed with real-
ities, takes refuge in fantasy at times, and that is un-

doubtedly what has happened to me. You may also be the result of vitamin shortage. That sometimes has a good deal to do with it. However, if I close my eyes and breathe deeply, you will undoubtedly disappear."

He closed his eyes, took two or three deep breaths and opened them again furtively. But the two men at arms were still there, still clad in surcoats and mail, and still staring at him out of hostile blue eyes.

"So," said Dr. Kokintz. "It is not a hallucination and I am a prisoner of war. But perhaps the matter will resolve itself if subjected to reason. Please tell me: who is the United States at war with?"

"The duchy of Grand Fenwick," replied Tully.

"The duchy of Grand Fenwick," repeated the doctor. He said the words quite slowly as if weighing them, to see whether they had any substance. "Certainly this is a hallucination," he concluded. "I was born in the duchy of Grand Fenwick. How can I be a prisoner of war of the place where I was born?"

"Look," said Tully grimly, conscious of the passing of the minutes. "This is not a hallucination. This is deadly earnest. The duchy of Grand Fenwick declared war on the United States over two months ago. We have invaded New York. You are our prisoner, and we are going to take you back to Grand Fenwick with us."

"But why did the duchy of Grand Fenwick declare war on the United States?" Dr. Kokintz asked.

"Over wine," replied Will. "You Americans are imitating our wine, putting out some kind of a rotgut brew and calling it Pinot Grand Enwick. That's why."

"Over wine," said Kokintz. "For what other reason would one expect a nation to go to war with the United States?" He shrugged his shoulders as if the matter was now entirely clear.

"Enough of this," rapped Tully. "You're coming with us as a prisoner of war. You and that bomb you made. Where is the bomb?"

"Bomb?" said the doctor, the word pulling him sharply to his senses out of the dream into which he felt he had slipped. "Bomb? What bomb are you talking about? I don't know of any bomb."

"This bomb here," said Tully, thrusting the copy of the *New York Times* in front of him. "The one that will blow up everything if it is exploded."

The physicist glanced for one second from them to the lead box on the bench. Suddenly he made a grab at it, but Tully was there before him and snatched the oblong container up in his big hand.

"Is this it?" he asked triumphantly. He thrust it out at arm's length, and the weight was such that he nearly dropped it. Indeed, it was slipping from his hand when he caught it with the other, letting his sword clatter to the floor to do so. Dr. Kokintz rose to his toes like a ballet dancer, and then subsided, his eyes closed tight behind his thick glasses.

"Please," he said, wiping a hand across his forehead. "Please be very careful. That box you have in your hand is dangerous."

"Is this the bomb?" Tully repeated, shaking it a little in emphasis.

"Please," pleaded Kokintz. "Careful. Handle it as if it were a baby mouse. Yes. That is the bomb. If you shake it like that, or rattle it, or drop it, or jar it, or disturb it in any way, it is likely to explode. And if it explodes it will blow up all of New York and Philadelphia and Boston. It will kill every living soul for several hundred miles around. And over and above that, it will release a dreadful gas which will keep on killing everything it comes in touch with for years and years to come. So I beg of you, put it down gently and spare the lives of millions of innocent people."

Will had been watching the scene with growing suspicion. He did not know what all this talk of a bomb was about. But if Tully said there was a bomb, then there must be a bomb. On the other hand it was hard to believe that the box his leader held in his hand could wipe out the whole of Grand Fenwick and more, which was what this Dr. Kokintz was trying to say.

He raised his sword now and reached for the bomb.

"Give it to me," he said, "and I'll cut it open and see what's inside. I think this man is lying, and that thing, which even if it was filled with gunpowder wouldn't wreck much more than this room, has got nothing in it but earth or sand."

"No! No!" screamed Dr. Kokintz. "No. Please. I beg of you. Don't hit it." He flung himself on Will and seized his sword arm in both hands.

"I don't think he is lying," said Tully quietly. "I think this is it. We ought to be going, but there's just one thing I want to ask. Why did you make this?" And he held the box contemptuously out towards the scientist.

"It is a peace weapon of the United States of America," Dr. Kokintz replied. "The only peace weapon of its kind; far more effective than the atom bomb or any other peace weapon devised so far."

"A peace weapon?" said Tully in some surprise, turning the box over in his hand. He looked over at Will who was leaning on his broadsword. "Well," he continued, "the sword Will there is leaning on is a peace weapon, only of course it's not as good as this one because you can't kill so many people with it. You know we in Grand Fenwick, being a small country, need a really good peace weapon, which is another reason for taking this contraption along with us. So let's go. Down the stairs. March."

Dr. Kokintz shrugged and walked to the door. But when he got there he turned around.

"What about my canary?" he said. "There will be no one to look after it."

"There won't be much need for anyone to look after it," replied Tully. "This city is going to be atom bombed pretty soon. Someone else using a peace weapon, and the sooner we get out of here, the better."

"Atom bombed!" exclaimed Will and Kokintz together.

"That's right. Read this." Tully showed them the *New York Times* again, pointing out the sentence on the front page which stated that the alert of the whole east coast of the United States, in preparation for atomic attack, was likely to be held in the next twenty-four hours. "The alert's on," he said, "so the attack should take place any minute."

"But this is only a practice alert," expostulated Kokintz. "The air-raid warden told me so. There is not going to be any real attack."

Tully looked at him hard for a second and then read the story again. It didn't say definitely that there was going to be a real atomic attack. In fact the deeper he read into it, the more evident it became that the alert was for practice only.

"Maybe you're right," he agreed at length, "and if so I'm much relieved about it. But while this practice alert is on we have still to get down to the *Endeavor* and get you out of here with this bomb. So, march."

"But my canary," said the doctor.

"Take your canary with you. But hurry," Tully ordered.

Kokintz snatched up the cage and walked swiftly out of the room. At the head of the stairs he turned to Tully. "Do not stumble and fall," he said. "Otherwise all New York will fall with you."

11

THERE WAS ONLY ONE CONFLICT WORTHY OF NOTE IN THE
victorious war of the duchy of Grand Fenwick against
the United States of America. And that was so small,
both in point of view of the numbers engaged and the
area fought over, that it is difficult to find a word to describe it which would satisfy the military student or in-
form the layman. "Battle" certainly would not do. "Engagement" is too vague. "Affray at arms" has too large
a ring to it. "Sortie" perhaps would best serve, for it was
undoubtedly a sortie, a breaking out of one force to
thrust through another and win its way to freedom.

Although the affair was minute, measured both in
terms of the forces engaged on both sides and the casualties sustained, yet it must rank in importance among the
major engagements of the world. For in the course of
this action, the lives of many millions of Americans were
saved—and saved, as the result of a peculiar irony, by
the invading side. And at the same time, the affair provided the invaders with the means of retreating brilliant-
ly from the field to return to their own country, their
objective achieved and their enemy defeated, though the
fact of their defeat was not appreciated by the Americans
for some time.

At the corner of One Hundred and Tenth Street and
Broadway, on their march downtown to return to the
brig *Endeavor*, having with them Dr. Kokintz and the
quadium bomb, the forces of Grand Fenwick, under
Tully, were met by the forces of the United States, led
by General Snippett, Commander of Civil Defense for
the New York area. General Snippett had under his
command his chauffeur, two sound trucks with armed
police seated beside the drivers and a mobile canteen
with a staff of four which had been reinforced by the

addition of two more armed policemen. His total force then was twelve, but it was mechanized, being contained in four automobiles.

The two armies, if the word is permissible, sighted each other from a distance, the streets being clear of all traffic, and at a range of five hundred yards commenced to dispose themselves for battle. The Fenwickians, following the style of defense developed towards the end of the fourteenth century, spread themselves across the avenue in a harrow formation. The gaps in the front line of bowmen were filled by a second line of men standing two paces behind them. Behind these, and covering the gaps in the second line, was a third line of warriors. On each side of this harrow formation the men at arms placed themselves to deal, with their broadswords and maces, with any attempt at a flanking movement. A flanking movement was not likely to develop, for the buildings on either side of the street would have proved too great an obstacle.

What General Snippett might have done was to go down a side street and, by executing three right-angle turns, take the Fenwick force in the rear. He did not realize this, however, until the assault was already well launched.

Seeing the invaders prepared for battle, General Snippett gallantly signaled his whole force to come to a standstill, took one armed policeman aboard his car, and advanced for a parley without further escort.

His chauffeur drove the car slowly to within a few hundred yards of the invaders and stopped. The car was a convertible with the top down, and when it had stopped, General Snippett rose in the front seat, and hailing the Fenwickians called out, "What the hell is all this about? Why aren't you down in the shelters?"

To this Tully replied courteously that he was the commander of the Grand Fenwick expeditionary force, which was at war with the United States, and offered General Snippett the opportunity of withdrawing honorably from the field since he was outnumbered. If, however, he refused to withdraw, Tully pointed out, there would be no alternative but to join battle, though every effort would be made to spare as many lives as possible.

General Snippett's reply to this was profane and very little to the point. He concluded by shouting out that if what he termed "that gang of idiots" wasn't on its way to an air-raid shelter in one minute, he would order his men to fire upon them.

Tully assumed that this being an ultimatum, the parley had concluded, and he gave the order for his bowmen to prepare to loose a volley, the target being the three other automobiles which had remained in the American lines five hundred yards away. When he saw the arrows flash in the sunlight as they were pulled from their quivers, watched them being fitted to the bow-strings, saw the bows raised slowly and then bent as each bowman leaned his left arm into the bow so as to bring his arm straight with his shoulder—when he saw all this, General Snippett appears to have lost his head.

He was heard to shout to the policeman with him, "Knock over that tall guy in the fancy-dress costume for me."

The policeman, who had a carbine with him, got out of the car for better aim and Tully called to Will, "Take off the fellow's hat. He lacks respect."

There was hardly a noticeable movement, hardly as much as the taking of aim, before the arrow sped from Will's bow like an angry bee. The policeman had only just raised his carbine when the yard-long shaft lanced through his hat, whipped it off his head and carried it a further hundred feet down the street before plunging into the asphalt. The shaft remained there, standing at an angle, the policeman's hat dangling from it, as the first trophy of war for Grand Fenwick.

The policeman himself fired at the moment that the arrow struck, but his aim was entirely spoiled and his round flung upwards at least twenty yards over Tully's head. Tully in the meantime took a bow from the man nearest him, and with the same casual unconcern displayed by Will, looking almost away from his target, whipped off General Snippett's hat with an arrow. This shaft also continued down the street to drop within a few feet of that fired by Will.

It was this last arrow, fired by Tully, which was unwittingly the cause of placing the lives of some millions of people, unconscious all of them of the battle, in jeopardy. For in order to take the bow, Tully had passed the quadium bomb to the bowman to hold, and the latter, unconscious of its true nature, paid it scant attention. In the minutes that followed, Tully himself forgot about the bomb. He knew, with an instinct for military tactics bred in him through the generations, that this was exactly the right moment to strike a vital blow at the enemy.

"One flight," he cried, "fifty feet this side of their lines. And then charge with sword and buckler."

The volley sped like a shower of hail down the street —a small compact bundle of arching arrows which threw a leaping shadow along the buildings, reached their zenith and then slipped down to the earth to thud into the road surface a few feet from the cars drawn up behind General Snippett. The arrows had hardly left the bowstrings before the men of Grand Fenwick had drawn their swords and, with bucklers thrust before them, hurled down upon General Snippett's car and the others to the rear. The general's automobile was quickly captured by Will, who jerked the chauffeur out of the seat and snatched the carbine away from the policeman and flung it through the window of a nearby building. He then fetched the general himself a cuff which, gallant man though he was, put him out of action for the remainder of the encounter.

The three cars composing the main American lines, however, were not so readily dealt with. The occupants of one, the canteen car, seeing a howling mob of men descending upon them, swords wheeling in bright circles in the sunlight, fled. The two policemen, however, stood their ground though uncertain for a second what to do. One raised his carbine and fired a shot which struck one of the Fenwick bowmen in the chest. The bowman fell, got up, and fell again, to remain quiet and still upon the street. He was a small farmer named Tom Cobley, a man of forty-five years of age, and that day he achieved more honor than had come to any of his countrymen in five centuries. For Tom Cobley was the first to die for Grand Fenwick in over five hundred years. His body, pickled in a barrel of brine, was later taken to his homeland and buried in a crypt next to that of Sir Roger Fenwick, in the heart of Fenwick Castle.

The stout defense of the American policeman was sufficient to give heart to the remainder of his comrades, who commenced to fire into the approaching horde. But there was no time for the Americans to aim, and the bowmen were upon them before they could loose more than two or three ineffective rounds. In the short melee that followed, the Fenwickian soldier who had been given the quadium bomb to carry, being because of his burden deprived of the use of any other wapon, decided to hurl it at one of his opponents. His arm was jostled as he threw, so the bomb flipped up in the air for about twenty feet. Tully caught a glimpse of it as it sped upward. He was standing on the hood of one of the automobiles perhaps ten feet from where it would fall and, in falling, destroy most of the major cities on the east coast of America.

He flung himself forward towards it, grasped it in his two hands as it came down, and rolled to the ground, the bomb held firmly to his chest. When he got up, New York and all its inhabitants had been saved, the forces of Grand Fenwick had won a decisive victory over their enemies and were in possession of their four automobiles; and Dr. Kokintz, who had been entrusted to the care of two men, had fainted. It was some minutes before he could be revived, and when his consciousness was restored, he took one look at the quadium bomb, which Tully held reassuringly before him, and fainted again.

The battle had lasted no more than five minutes from the initial parley with General Snippett to the capture of all the American equipment plus the general himself, his chauffeur, and four policemen. The remainder of the American force had fled the field, and Tully ordered his men to get into the American cars, and follow him down to the Cunard dock where the brig *Endeavor* awaited them. Since Tully was the only man in Grand Fenwick who knew how to handle an automobile, the other cars were driven by the captured Americans, swords pressed to their sides to ensure that they attempted no escape.

During the journey to the dock, General Snippett recovered consciousness to demand what the hell everybody thought they were doing.

"You'll pay for this with the rest of your lives in jail," he thundered. "Let me out of here, or I'll call all the cops in New York out after you." After he had fumed for a while without anyone paying any attention, he assumed a more reasonable tone and asked once again what it was all about.

Tully explained to him patiently that he was a prisoner of war of the duchy of Grand Fenwick, that he would be taken back to Grand Fenwick, treated according to his rank which he judged to be that of a captain, and held there for ransom according to the procedures of civilized nations. This produced another explosion from the general and when he had again subsided, he asked what or where was the duchy of Grand Fenwick, and what was the cause of the war.

The reply to this, that the duchy was an independent nation five miles long and three wide, contained in the northern slopes of the Alps, and that the war had been brought about as a result of the enterprise of some California wine makers, reduced the general to a stunned silence, for which Tully was grateful, for he had a number of things to think about and only a short while in which to make his decision.

His first problem was to get Dr. Kokintz and the quadium bomb to Grand Fenwick safely. The only transportation at his disposal was the brig, which would take three weeks at least to get to the port nearest to the duchy. In that three weeks it might be set upon in the high seas and sunk by American craft since a state of war existed between the two countries. He toyed with the idea of driving to the nearest airfield and commandeering a plane to fly the doctor and the bomb to Grand Fenwick.

But there were potent arguments against such a plan. In the first place, it might prove impossible to find a plane and a pilot capable of making the transatlantic flight. In the second place, they might encounter in the drive to the nearest airfield, which he judged to be Idlewild, such superior forces of the enemy that he would be unable to defeat them.

He decided to trust to the brig. Despite the fact that it was almost incapable of defense, and would take so long to reach a home port, there was one factor in their favor. And that was the strange circumstance that the United States apparently did not know that it was at war with Grand Fenwick. Indeed, Tully now doubted that more than a handful of people in New York were aware that an invasion force had entered the city, marched to Columbia University, breached the building and stolen the most valuable military secret which the United States possessed. Thus there was a strong possibility that all would arrive safely home in the duchy before the truth was discovered.

The next point was whether he should remain with some of the men to carry out the original plan for an attack upon the White House and the seizure of the President. He decided against this. It was, he argued, unnecessary. The Fenwick forces had already seized in the person of Dr. Kokintz and the quadium bomb far greater booty, far more capable of bringing the United States to terms, than the person of the President.

Thinking of Dr. Kokintz he was reminded that the scientist had said he was from Grand Fenwick. Tully turned to Will, who sat on the other side of the general's car, the general being between them.

"Will," he said, "do you ever recall a family by the name of Kokintz in Grand Fenwick?"

Will thought solemnly upon the matter for a minute or two. "I don't remember them myself," he said at length, "but my father once spoke of some people called Kokintz. There was a man and a woman. They were gypsy folk, traveling through, and the woman was pregnant and couldn't go any further. The two were permitted to stay in Grand Fenwick until the baby was born.

"My father said the woman died, and the duke took pity on the man and said he could remain in the duchy as long as he pleased. He stayed about three years or maybe more, then he left, I believe for America, taking his son with him. That's all I ever heard of it."

"The name seems more familiar than that to me," said Tully. He looked at the doctor, who was sitting between guards in the back seat of the convertible. He had the cage with his canary on his lap and was talking to the bird.

"That's it," said Tully suddenly. "Birds. Kokintz is the man who challenged my father when he wrote his book about the native birds of Grand Fenwick. He said that Grand Fenwick was too small to have any native birds. I remember now. Hey, you," he called to the scientist, "didn't you once write a paper saying that there were no native birds in Grand Fenwick?"

"I did," Kokintz replied mildly.

"Well, you'll soon have an opportunity to correct your error," Tully said grimly. "You'll learn all about the native birds of Grand Fenwick starting with this one"—he pointed to the double-headed eagle on his surcoat—"and ending up with sparrows. Sparrows in Grand Fenwick have a tuft of feathers on the top of their heads."

"Probably nuthatches," said Dr. Kokintz, blinking through his thick glasses.

"You can call them nuthatches if you like over here," retorted Tully, "or eagles if you want to. But in Grand Fenwick they're sparrows and they have a tuft of feathers on the top of their heads."

By this time they had arrived at the Cunard dock. Pedro and his crew of five were lolling around the deck, dozing in the spring sun. A hail from Tully brought them quickly to their feet.

"We're coming aboard," he said. "Prepare to cast off and make sail."

"How about a few hours' shore leave?" asked Pedro. "Some of the boys haven't seen an American girl in four or five years."

"Cast off," roared Tully, "this is no time to think of wenching."

Pedro shrugged and signaled to the men who commenced to busy themselves with the fore and aft moorings. Dr. Kokintz, the general, the four policemen and the chauffeur were hustled down ropes to the deck of the brig and then put below in the main cabin. The rest of the Grand Fenwick force followed them. Tully remained alone on the dock after they were all aboard.

"Stand by until I come down," he said. "There is one thing more for me to do." He took a grappling iron on the end of the rope and flung it to the roof of an adjoining building. On top was a flagstaff displaying the Stars and Stripes. This he lowered and bundled under his arm. Then he bent on the banner of Grand Fenwick, with the eagle which said "Aye," from one beak and "Nay" from the other, and raised it to the top of the staff.

He then returned to the brig which cast off and was soon running under all plain sail down the river.

Pedro at the wheel, still disgruntled that his crew had been denied shore leave in the sailor's paradise of New York, said sarcastically, "Well, you were away about five hours. How did the war with the United States go?"

"We won," said Tully calmly. Pedro was so surprised he swallowed his quid of chewing tobacco.

12

THE SECRETARY OF DEFENSE DECIDED TO CALL OFF THE
great air-raid alert of the east coast after only six hours,
and that for a number of reasons. The most potent of
these was that the people would not stand for it lasting
any longer, and he really had no choice in the matter.
No portion of a nation, which in all its long history had
been dedicated to individualism, to the proposition that
there should be the least amount of law to govern the
greatest number of people, would submit to being arbi-
trarily and indefinitely shut up in houses and in cellars,
in subways and in shelters, forbidden the comforts of radios, of television, of refrigerators and iced drinks, of
cups of coffee and of slugs of whisky or glasses of beer.
Risk of death after a while became preferable to this,
which was, for such a people, a form of living death.
Mothers who had been separated from their children
stood the separation for two hours and then would stand
it no more. All the pleadings of wardens, all the threats
of police, all the appeals to their patriotism and the assurance that their offspring were being as well cared for
as if they were in their own homes would not solace
them. At the risk of being reduced to a spoonful of
ashes on the moment, they left their homes, to demand,
with that appalling anger of which only women are
capable, to be taken to their children immediately.

Against their wrath, the forces of the Civil Defense
Organization were of no avail. The women won, and in
the suburbs and residential areas, the air-raid alert
though still officially on, faded gradually away. This happened not only in the New York area, but in Boston and
Philadelphia and Washington, D.C. and Providence,
Rhode Island. For the first time in the history of the

United States, if not in the world, women, in effect, canceled a war.

The rebellion was slower in getting started in the downtown areas of the cities, where most of those caught in the air raid were men. Perhaps because generations of active participation in warfare had conditioned men to the necessity for being herded, it was three or four hours before there was any active rebellion against being enclosed in places of safety. In New York there had been the rumor that the city was being invaded by men from Mars, who had landed in flying saucers. The first effect of this, as already told, was panic. The panic was followed by a kind of false courage, or bravado, manifested in the singing of "Mairzy Doats," "The Little Doggie in the Window," and "Abide with Me" in the subways. This turned to impatience that nothing appeared to be happening. And the impatience became, in a little while, active rebellion in which those in the subways demanded to be let out to go to their homes.

The Secretary of Defense had done all he could to keep the situation in New York under control, even to dispatching his Civil Defense Chief, General Snippett, to put down the rumor about the men from Mars. But three hours after he had sent him on this mission, there was still no report from General Snippett. And still the anguished appeals of other defense officials poured in, stating that the population was getting completely out of hand.

At the Eighty-sixth Street West Side subway, a group of men started looting a train which had stopped there. They dismantled most of the motor and ripped up the seat cushions. Attempts to prevent them were blocked by others who were taking no active part in the looting. It seemed that New Yorkers who had long traveled on the subways bore some kind of grudge against the dinginess and noisiness of the trains and were seizing this opportunity to get a kind of revenge for their years of suffering and crowding.

On the East Side, at the Seventy-seventh Street station, a train had been derailed. Mustaches had been drawn on every poster in the station which bore a human face, whether male or female, and by a strange coincidence, those who had been caught by the sirens at Fifty-ninth Street were short of cigarettes. There were, the wardens reported, about five hundred people in the station and no more than twenty packs of cigarettes. These had quickly been disposed of and the whole mob had taken up the chant, "I'd brave an atomic pile for a Camel." This was followed by the whole five hundred roaring, "Call for Philip Morris," the drawn-out cry echoing down the dark and silent tunnels and off the iron stanchions and girders.

There were a dozen other symptoms of impending revolt of a like nature to be reported, not only from New York but also from other cities. The plain fact of the matter was that there were too few officials to control the crowds. And the crowds, individually and collectively, would prefer to meet their fate in the open than be kept penned up in safety.

That was the general situation which brought about the cancellation after six hours of a monster air-raid alert which was to have lasted much longer. There were particular reasons, however, why the Secretary of Defense decided to call off the exercise.

The first and the most perplexing of these was the disappearance of General Snippett. When he did not report back three hours after being sent out to deal with the rumor of the men from Mars, the secretary called the general's headquarters in New York and sent out a search party for him. The search party, consisting of two hundred policemen on motorcycles, took every avenue and parallel street on Manhattan Island from the Battery to the Bronx. But no sign of the general was to be found. His car, with two sound trucks and a mobile canteen, was, however, discovered at the Cunard dock. There were several dents in the body and most mysterious of all, an arrow, three feet long, embedded in the upholstery of the back seat. When this report was turned in, the secretary ordered all four cars taken to the police garage and kept there until he had a chance to inspect them personally. On second thought, he asked that the arrow be sent to him immediately by special messenger.

The police turned in one further report, though this was not until some time later. This was to the effect that the main door of the administration building of Columbia University had been smashed in, apparently by a battering ram made of a tree which had been cut down nearby.

The final argument, if indeed one was necessary, for the cancellation of the alert, was pressure from the east coast press. With the whole of their readership locked up, with their circulation, printing, typesetting departments unable to get to work, or to work even if they were already in their offices, newspaper publishers were unable to bring out their editions and were in danger of losing large sums of money for an indefinite period.

In New York the editors of the *Times*, the *Herald Tribune*, the *Daily Mirror*, the *Daily News*, the *Journal-American*, the *Compass*, the *Post* and the *World-Telegram and Sun* met in defiance of the air-raid restrictions at Bleeck's bar on Thirty-ninth Street, and putting aside their policy differences and professional criticisms the one of the other, solemnly vowed that they would have the scalp of the Secretary of Defense unless the air raid was canceled and their readership returned to them.

"Unless we have a freely circulating daily press, we have lost whatever war we are fighting or are called upon to fight," the editor of the *Times* announced. "It is one thing if people are prevented from reading newspapers because they have been killed by an atom bomb, but quite another thing if they are prevented from reading newspapers for fear of being killed by an atom bomb."

The editor of the *Daily Mirror* made a note of this on the back of an envelope and ran a box in the first post-air-raid edition to appear summarizing the *Times* editor's remarks under the headline: TIMES CLAIMS PRECEDENCE OVER A-BOMB.

So the great alert was canceled and the confusion which followed was almost as chaotic as that which preceded it. The telephone exchanges were overwhelmed as a liberated population called relatives, newspapers, fire stations, police stations, radio stations, television stations, indeed all sources of information to inquire whether all was well, whether the men from Mars had withdrawn, whether it was true that Manhattan was a shambles, and whether it was true that all the water had been rendered radioactive by agents ranging from atomic explosives to fiery darts hurled from the silent reaches of space. Those in the cities sought to go to their homes; those in their homes in the suburbs, seized by an irresistible curiosity, sought to get to the cities—in Boston to view the reported shambles of Old North Church; in Philadelphia to examine the wreckage of Independence Hall; in New York to gaze with horror and wonder on what report had it was the blackened skeleton of the world's proudest city.

Thus thousands of families missed their immediate reunion, adding to the confusion. Reports of missing persons turned in by distraught husbands and wives ran into tens of thousands. The police, the Civil Defense Organization, the Red Cross, the Traveler's Aid—all were quite unable to cope with them. And in this morass of rumor and of inquiry, of hysteria and of bustling about from one place to another, Mrs. Reiner's report that her boarder, Dr. Kokintz, had not been home for three days and was not to be found anywhere, was utterly lost.

Mrs. Reiner, however, had not spent fifty-five years living in Brooklyn to have her own aims and interest set aside or swallowed in a furor involving millions.

"You find Mr. Kokintz," she instructed the Missing Persons Bureau, Manhattan Division, "or I come over there and find him myself. What for you think I pay taxes?"

"Lady," said the weary clerk to whom her call had been switched, "we got maybe ten thousand people reported missing in the last three hours. Four of our own men in the Missing Persons Bureau is missing and there ain't nowhere we can report them to. How do you spell his name?"

"Kokintz," said Mrs. Reiner. "Anybody knows how to

spell Kokintz. It's a natural name, easy to spell, like Schmidt."

"Well," replied the clerk, "maybe I might spell it wrong. You spell it for me."

"Look," said Mrs. Reiner, "I'm not spending ten cents calling you for you to get fresh about my spelling. Kokintz is the name. A very nice bachelor gentleman that sometimes stays out at night. Working at the Columbia University, he says. But he never stayed out two nights and three days before."

"We'll look for him," replied the clerk, "and let you know what we find." He hung up and filled out a routine report saying that a Mr. Kokenz, bachelor, aged about fifty, wearing thick glasses, bird lover, fond of staying out at night, was missing. He put the form with twenty others he had filled out in the past hour and turned to the next call.

Mrs. Reiner, however, was not satisfied. She had already called Dr. Kokintz at his special number at the university, the private line whose secret she shared with the President of the United States, and got no reply. She debated whether she should go over to Columbia and make inquiries personally. But she had other boarders to look after, and there was a quantity of grocery shopping to do for them. She did her shopping, fretting the while, and then decided that she would write a letter to the President about her missing boarder.

The letter took her a full hour to compose, but she felt the time was well spent when she was finished. It read:

DEAR PRESIDENT OF THESE UNITED STATES:

Mr. Kokintz, my boarder, has been missing three days and two nights now, and I want you should help to find him. He is a bachelor gentleman and sometimes stays out at night, but never as much as this before. Sometimes he says he is out because he is working and sometimes he says he fell asleep in a movie. I been feeding his birds while he is away and I will keep on feeding them, natch. But I am worried about him. He is a nice gentleman and pays his rent regular and I am worried about him. So please help me find him. Maybe you got people can search the movie houses. Some of them are open twenty-four hours a day and there may be a lot of missing people in there.

Your fellow citizen
ELIZA REINER

P.S. I voted Republican all my life except when we needed a Democrat during the depression.

The letter, due to the disruption of the postal services and the fact that Mrs. Reiner had addressed it merely "The President of These United States," was four days arriving at the White House and another three days before it reached—after examination by the secret service—the desk of the secretary who culled the correspondence which should be brought to the attention of the Chief Executive. He decided on a whim to let the President see it, not that it was important but because it might cheer him up with its humanity.

In the meantime, a number of strange oddments arising out of the great alert were uncovered. But they were all of them lost for several days in the great welter of news which the exercise had engendered. A *New York Herald Tribune* reporter, covering the waterfront, discovered a banner with a double-headed eagle flying atop a customs shed in the place of the Stars and Stripes. Nobody knew who put it there. Nobody knew what it represented. It developed that the Stars and Stripes was supposed to be raised at dawn each day and lowered at sunset. But the man whose duty it was to attend to this was among the missing of the great exercise—he turned up later in Toronto, Canada, indignantly pointing out that he had gone away on his regularly scheduled annual leave. In the confusion, his replacement had forgotten about the flag-raising ceremony.

The reporter turned in the story and it was put down as some kind of a hoax, a hoax which, as the *Tribune* pointed out in a small and dignified editorial, was in the poorest of taste. The item, however, came to the attention of the Secretary of Defense and he sent for the double-headed eagle banner in the same way that he had sent for the three-foot arrow found in the back of the missing General Snippett's car.

Then, three days after the alert, the press got around to reporting that the main doors of Columbia University had been beaten open with an improvised battering ram. Nothing inside, however, had been touched. The incident was again taken to be some kind of irresponsible frolic indulged in by parties unknown. One theory was that a number of would-be students, whose candidacies had been refused because the university was full, had battered down the doors to illustrate their determination to be admitted. The dean made scrupulous and intensive inquiries and satisfied himself that the incident could not be laid to any of his students. In a statement issued to the press, he deplored the barbarism of those who had cut down a tree to smash open the university doors and had compounded their crime by apparently taking a coat of fine chain mail of the fourteenth century out of some museum to make a head for their battering ram.

"Armor of this kind is exceedingly rare," his statement read. "The mail used was a hauberk, or shirt of chain, covering the head, neck, shoulders, and whole figure of a man. Many sections have been irreparably damaged."

But an armorer employed by the Metropolitan Museum, who asked permission to examine the suit, declared that he believed he knew of every piece of chain mail in the United States and this was not one of them. "This suit of mail," he told the dean, "is made on the exact pattern of the fourteenth century, but judging by its condition it has either been remarkably well preserved, or was made much later by an expert armorer. The only place in the world today where such armorers are to be found is in the duchy of Grand Fenwick."

The statement by the chain-mail expert was reported in the *Times*, which obtained an exclusive on the story, and this also came to the attention of the Secretary of Defense. He sent for the hauberk in the same way he had sent for the arrow and the eagle banner. Then he

went to the *Encyclopaedia Britannica* and read all there
was available on the duchy of Grand Fenwick. There
were only five lines, giving a desiccated history. One of
the lines said that the national flag was a double-headed
eagle banner. The secretary became so absorbed in the
discovery that he forgot to leave his office at 5:30 that
evening—the first time he had been guilty of staying late
in twenty years of government service.

All this detail, however, bizarre though it was and excellent newspaper copy in normal times, was largely lost
to the press and the general public in the spate of other
news concerning the great alert. The first two days' issues
of the east coast press were devoted to overall coverage
of the exercise, to interviews with officials all of whom
chorused that the alert had proved to the hilt the capacity of the people to respond correctly in time of an emergency, to reporting such incidents—somewhat in contra-
diction of the official statements—as the looting of the
train on the West Side subway, the singing in the underground stations, the excellent work of the volunteer defense workers, and stories of children, mothers, and
fathers who had performed acts of fortitude or whimsy
during the exercise.

A Civil Defense worker who had reunited a boy in
the Bronx with his lost dog came in for special commen-
dation. Another who had supplied three gallons of ice
cream to the inmates of a Queens orphanage was a hero
for twenty-four hours. A child born in the basement of
the Waldorf-Astoria was christened Waldorf Blitz Cun-
ningham; its parents were made guests of the hotel for
a month and showered with ten thousand dollars' worth
of layettes until the mother wrote a letter thanking everybody and begging mothers not to send any more diapers
or Pablum because there was nowhere to store the quantity already received.

As a matter almost of duty, the press, with the exception of the *New York Daily News,* united to assure the
public that there had been no invasion of men from
Mars in flying saucers, and deplored those rumor-

mongers who had come close to jeopardizing the success of the exercise by spreading such a story.

When he read this, Tom Mulligan, leader of Civil Defense Section 4-300, subsection 3, decontamination, who had now been relieved of his duties for turning in a report of an invasion from space, collected two or three of his former section men together. He made a short and bitter address to them, in the privacy of his own home, in which he pointed out that they were being made to look like fools by higher officials of the Civil Defense Organization, who refused to believe that they had met with and been attacked by men clad in metal suits during the great alert.

"Now," said Tom. "Answer me plain. Did you or did you not see a bunch of guys on Broadway dressed up in some kind of shiny clothes?"

The men of his section agreed that they undoubtedly had.

"And," continued Tom, "didn't they throw some kind of a ray or something at us that whistled when it went by?"

There was some disagreement as to whether the weapon had been a ray, but none whatever that something had been thrown at them which whistled as it went by.

"As patriotic Americans then," said Tom, "it's our duty to get the facts before the public. It's my belief that these invaders from Mars"—nothing would shake his opinion that the men in shinys suits came from outer space—"are still around. And they're probably killing people right and left without anybody knowing it. The brass"—and the way he said the word was a full indictment of all officialdom—"is trying to cover up. They don't want the people to know. They don't want 'em to know that they failed in trying to keep the spacemen out. But we've got to get the facts out. And the way to do it, since nobody will listen to us, is go down to the *Daily News* and tell them about it. They'll print the truth—promise to do it right on one of their pages."

The others, after being deprived of their jobs in Civil

Defense, and thrust unceremoniously, just like civilians, into the subway shelter, were not enthusiastic. One argued that if the brass was covering up, they might have a good reason for doing so. Another said that if they hadn't been believed by their own outfit, there wasn't much likelihood that they'd be believed by a newspaper. But Tom was not to be so readily blocked. He said he knew someone on the *Daily News*, an important man, and he would listen to them and see that their story got into the newspaper.

Tom was stretching the facts a little when he said he knew someone of importance on the *Daily News*. The person he knew was a district circulation manager for whom he had sold papers on commission for six or seven months. He was hard to get to, but Tom persisted, and after he had told him his story, the district circulation manager asked one question.

"Did you say this happened uptown?"

"Yes," said Tom. "Hundredth and Broadway."

"Could do with a few more sales around the West Hundreds," the circulation manager said, half to himself. "Tell you what, I'll call the city editor and tell him you're coming down. Give him that men from Mars angle strong. That's pretty good: MARTIANS LAND UPTOWN. Worth an extra, if he'll go for it. Remember you got to give him your name and be quoted as a defense worker. Right?"

"Right," said Tom.

Down he went with his three section workers, considerably heartened, to the *Daily News* office on the East Side. They saw the city editor for two fast minutes and he seemed almost angry that they hadn't got any pictures. He turned them over to a reporter, a thin, earnest, bespectacled young man who asked so many questions on minor details that Tom had a suspicion he had been planted in the *Daily News* office by the very brass who were out to keep the story under wraps. But he answered all the questions he could, and signed a broad statement covering the story. The men who were with him signed the statement too. Then they went home.

"Tomorrow it will be all over the front page," Tom said.

It wasn't.

The reporter turned in his story, and the city editor read it through torn between caution and exultation. He wanted to run it right then, but years of double-checking on statements held him back. He compromised by taking it into the managing editor, who gave it a fast run through.

"These guys swear to it," the city editor said. "We've checked their credentials and they're legit. They were with the Civil Defense Organization. And they did turn in a report of men from Mars. But the CDO says they were drunk and lost their decontamination suits and that's all there is to it. Swell story if we could figure out a way to run it without going out on a limb."

The managing editor put his feet on the desk and contemplated the toes of his shoes.

" 'Member that story *Tribune* ran other day in shirt-tail about funny flag on top of customs shed?" he asked. He had a habit of talking fast and leaving out what he regarded as superfluous syllables, articles and conjunctions.

"Yep," said the city editor.

"Funny thing," continued the managing editor. "Been trying get Snippett for coupla days for statement. Can't find him. Found car though." He took his feet suddenly off the desk and leaned forward in his chair. "Car's in police garage all busted up with hole in back seat. Get couple best men and turn them on it. Want story about disappearance Civil Defense Chief during alert, but car found all bust up."

"What about this men from Mars stuff?" the city editor asked.

"Throw them in too," said the managing editor, putting his feet back on the desk. "Here's what we got. General gone. Strange flag over customs house. General's car busted up like he'd been in fight. Defense worker reports invasion by men in shiny suits. Another thing, door Columbia bust open and some kind of steel shirt found on end battering ram. All adds up: MARTIANS INVADE MANHATTAN. DEFENSE CHIEF CAPTIVE. Let me see story when it's all in. And get this guy and his men back. Keep 'em hid away till we're out on street. They're ace in hole."

The city editor bustled out and beckoned two reporters over to his desk. They had a quick conference, were joined by two photographers and left the building.

13

"MR. PRESIDENT," SAID THE SECRETARY OF DEFENSE, "I ASKED for this private interview because I have a report to make which is almost unbelievable, but which is nonetheless true. It is so incredible a matter that it is hard to know exactly where to begin."

"Sit down," said the President with a smile, "and don't bother about where you are going to begin. Just tell me what you have on your mind."

"Well," said the secretary, "you will forgive me, I hope, if I seem to overemphasize the fact that every word I have to say is the truth. I stress this because I realize you will have great difficulty in crediting what follows. But I have not come to you before fully checking and rechecking all my conclusions."

The President gave him a puzzled look. "Go ahead," he said quietly.

The secretary swallowed hard. He was obviously under considerable strain and having difficulty in keeping his voice steady.

"Mr. President," he blurted out at length, "we are at war with another nation. We have been at war it would seem for some time, though we didn't know it. And furthermore we have been invaded by an expeditionary force of this nation which attacked New York City during the great alert and successfully withdrew after achieving its object.

"In fact, Mr. President, we are not only at war with this nation, but I believe that this nation has won the war. The United States has, for the first time in its history, been defeated."

"Good God," said the President. "Are you out of your mind?"

"No," said the Secretary of Defense, calmer now that

the biggest impact of this report had been delivered. "I am not out of my mind. It's all horribly true. I did not know that we were at war myself. In fact, I never suspected such a thing until some odd occurrences took place during the alert. At first I did not pay much attention to them. We were all still concerned with assessing the effect of the alert. However, certain remarkable irregularities were, as I say, brought to my attention. I asked the Treasury to let me have the use of two of their best secret service men. I requested them to investigate these happenings, to get all the details and background concerning them. Their report shows beyond a quibble that we are at war, that we have been invaded, and that we have in all probability lost the war. This," he added almost to himself, "is without a doubt the first war in world history in which secret service men had to be employed to find out that a war was going on."

The President got up from his desk, walked around it and stood before the Secretary of Defense, looking down at him.

"I'm not going to ask any questions about whether you are feeling well, because I believe you are," he said. "I'm not going to ask whether this is a joke because I know you have sufficient respect for the office of the President of the United States not to make a mockery of it. Now. Give me the facts. Who is this other nation? What did they do? When did they do it? And why did they do it? And above all, how do you arrive at the conclusion that they have won some kind of secret war with us? I am not aware that we are a conquered nation."

"Not conquered, Mr. President," said the Secretary of Defense. "But defeated." He reached down to the side of his chair and picked up a portfolio. "Can we go over to the desk?" he asked nervously.

The President nodded curtly and led the way.

The Secretary of Defense opened the portfolio and took out of it a scroll of paper which he unrolled on the desktop.

At the top was a double-headed eagle crest, the eagle

saying "Yea" out of one beak and "Nay" out of the other. Below in Old English lettering was the title "duchy of Grand Fenwick."

The President read the document through slowly and aloud. When he came to the final paragraph which ran, "therefore be it *Resolved*, The duchy of Grand Fenwick, having taken all steps it can to remedy the matter peaceably, does here and now, and by these presents, declare that a state of war exists between itself and the United States of America," he said solemnly and deliberately. "Damnedest thing I ever heard of." And he sat down slowly in his chair to stare at his Secretary of Defense.

The two sat looking at each other for perhaps thirty seconds without a word spoken. They both sensed that it was not a time for words. It was, rather, a time to try to capture each other's thoughts without resort to the use of the voice. But the thoughts were too jumbled. They ranged all the way from the catastrophic to the ridiculous. There was a need to pin them down and make sense of them. The President broke the silence.

"Give me that thing again," he said. The secretary gave him the declaration of war by the duchy of Grand Fenwick and he read it through once more.

"All right," said the President. "Now where did this come from? I presume that you have checked that it is a legitimate document?"

"I have," said the secretary. "And it is. It was found by the secret service in the apartment of a clerk named Chester X. Beston who works in the State Department. To be precise, it was found behind the radiator in his apartment."

"What the blazes was it doing there?" the President demanded, his face pink with anger.

"It wasn't really Beston's fault," the secretary replied hurriedly. "He works in the Central European Division. The document was delivered to him by routine messenger and when he opened it he thought it was just a joke by some of the boys in the pressroom. He put it in his pocket, went canoeing that evening and his canoe tipped over. He put the declaration of war down behind the radiator to dry out and forgot about it. The secret service men traced it after uncovering other evidence that we were at war with Grand Fenwick."

"What other evidence?" the President asked crisply.

The secretary told him, in short efficient sentences, the whole story of the reports of an invasion by men from Mars, the appearance in Manhattan of a group of men clad in armor, the disappearance of General Snippett, the finding of his car badly dented, with three others, at Pier 42, and the finding of the banner of Grand Fenwick flying over the customs shed on the waterfront.

"The secret service has checked these details thoroughly and there is no room for doubt that New York was invaded by Grand Fenwick during the alert. Why they should want to capture General Snippett, however, I do not know. I can only presume that his capture was accidental. I had sent him to suppress the rumors of an invasion from Mars which was causing panic in the New York subway. Probably he met with the Fenwick raiders and was taken prisoner. We found a three-foot arrow embedded in the upholstery of the back seat of his car. Four policemen are also missing. They must have been captured with him."

"A three-foot arrow?" the President asked, running a hand over his thinning hair.

"Yes," said the Secretary of Defense. "I suppose I should have explained that before. The duchy of Grand Fenwick hasn't fought a war since sometime in the fourteenth century. Their troops are armed and equipped just like the soldiers of the Hundred Years' War in Europe. They wear coats of mail and fight with longbows, maces, and lances . . ."

The President cut him short.

"You mean that we have been successfully invaded by fourteenth-century Europeans?"

"Yes," replied the secretary.

The President stood up and then sat down again. He closed his eyes and putting his elbows on his desk, clasped his head between his hands as if it were falling apart and had to be held together by physical force.

"I still don't get it," he said. "What was the object of this invasion?"

"The wine," replied the secretary patiently. "A wine maker in San Rafael, Marin County, California, started a close imitation of Pinot Grand Fenwick, which is the only export of the duchy. The people of Grand Fenwick saw their livelihood being threatened. I must admit that they had a point. Wars have been fought over similar causes through the centuries. The opium wars in China, for instance, and then the long warfare between the Dutch and the English over the Spice Islands."

"But this is the twentieth century," interrupted the President. "There are other means of righting these grievances short of warfare. We are a reasonable nation. We stand for peace. In fact, it is our policy to protect the weaker nations. Why did they have to go to war with us?"

"The trouble was that we're too big and they're too little," the secretary replied quietly. "They did try to settle the matter peacefully, as they say in their declaration of war. We have found an official communiqué from the duchy, signed by the Duchess Gloriana XII and addressed to the United States Chamber of Commerce, drawing attention to the manufacture of this imitation Pinot Grand Fenwick and asking that it be suppressed."

"What happened to that?" asked the President.

The secretary blushed. "It was forwarded to the vintners for comment and they used it for promotion purposes. They claimed in a series of advertisements of questionable taste that their product was so like the original Pinot that it had brought an official protest against its sale. They tied this claim in with some kind of blurb about American ingenuity improving on the centuries' old skill of European wine makers."

"Oh, no," said the President.

"Yes," said the secretary.

There was a little silence.

"Did the Grand Fenwick people do anything else?"

"Yes. There was another communiqué, also signed by Gloriana XII, to the Department of Agriculture, registering a protest against the sale of the imitation Pinot. This seems to have got lost in the shuffle. The only reply we can trace was the sending of a bulletin by the Department to the duchess. The bulletin was entitled 'Winemaking and the Culture of Grapes in California.'"

The President closed his eyes. "And then their formal declaration of war was first of all dunked in the Potomac and then put down behind a radiator to dry out," he said half to himself. "You know, I am beginning to sympathize with this duchy. Their biggest job seems to have been not to go to war but to get people to realize that they had a reason for going to war. And then, by golly, we had to use the secret service to find out that they had attacked us. How did they get over here?"

"That's something of a mystery. There are two theories. The first which seems the more probable is at the same time the most outlandish. That is that they somehow or other got hold of a submarine and came over on that. That would account for the complete disappearance of the general and the four policemen. If the sub came up the Hudson during the alert at periscope depth it would hardly be noticed. They could have landed from it, marched through Manhattan, captured the general and gone without more than a handful of persons knowing of it. And in the flurry of rumor, at the time, even those would not be believed.

"I don't believe the submarine story myself, however. A little nation like Grand Fenwick, completely landlocked, would hardly have a submarine and I don't know of anywhere you can charter one. The other theory is that they came over on a sailing vessel. There's some support for this in a curious story in the British press a week after the alert. The captain of the *Queen Mary*, which cleared New York just as the sirens sounded, gave an interview to reporters on the subject of the exercise when he arrived in England. He let drop that when he had got fairly to sea, he sighted a brig—that's a two-masted sailing vessel with square sails—hailed her and told her to put about as the Port of New York was closed. The brig continued on its course and he hailed her again. The only reply was a shower of arrows from the brig. Nobody was hurt."

The President picked up the declaration of war once again and read it through. He felt he was perhaps dreaming, or in some kind of a trance. Certainly it was difficult to grasp that this was reality, that the greatest republic in the world had been invaded by the smallest nation in the world and all without anybody knowing a thing about it.

"What do you mean," he asked, "when you say that Grand Fenwick won this war? You mean because they were able to invade us, take some hostages and get away again?"

"Yes," said the secretary. "When this thing gets out—and it's bound to get out—we'll be made the laughing-stock of the world. We'll lose prestige everywhere. Think what the Muscovites will make of this. A hand-ful of men from a tiny nation forced to invade the im-perialist capitalists to right their wrongs, and so on. The upholders of liberty trampling upon a tiny state, threat-ening them with starvation for capitalistic profits. It's all nonsense, but it'll make first-class propaganda to feed to their satellites. We'll lose heavily, very heavily in-deed, on the international scene. And no matter how many times we explain the thing and no matter in how much detail, it will be just that much worse. Some of the Latin American countries, you know, claim that while they have to listen to us, we never listen to them. And they'll point to the war by Grand Fenwick as a classic example of how far a little nation has to go to get a hearing from the United States.

"We lost all right. Just the very fact that Grand Fen-wick had to declare war against us lost us the war on the propaganda and prestige front."

The President sat staring at his desk top, quite bereft of anything to say which might be profitable. There were too many angles to the astounding news given him by the Secretary of Defense to select one on which to concentrate his thoughts. Almost without being conscious of what he was doing, he opened a portfolio on the desk which contained the incoming batch of documents for his attention.

He riffled through these moodily, pulled out those which he knew by experience required immediate attention. Towards the end of the stack he came upon a cheap little envelope on which were written in a round childish script the words, "To the President of These United States." He picked this up and opened it. The secretary, watching him, saw him become suddenly alert and tense as he read the letter which the envelope had contained.

When he had finished, the President reached swiftly for a telephone and snapped into the mouthpiece: "Get me Hoover at the FBI. Yes. In person." Then glancing up at the Secretary of Defense and covering the mouthpiece with his hand, he said: "Kokintz has gone. Disappeared. I don't know about the bomb. But if Grand Fenwick captured Kokintz and the quadium bomb we're licked. Completely. Grand Fenwick becomes the most powerful nation in the world."

14

THE COUNT OF MOUNTJOY WAS FOR SENDING THE THING back. He regarded the possession of the Q-bomb as in about the same category as someone importing an enormous and fiercely active volcano into Grand Fenwick and placing it right in the center of the duchy's fertile valleys to await its eruption.

"Your Grace," he told the duchess in a private audience shortly after Tully returned with Dr. Kokintz, the bomb, General Snippett, and four New York policemen, "we have fought a war against my better judgment and reaped, as the fruits of victory, incalculable disaster. This frightful engine which the man Bascomb has malignantly brought into our land may at the mere rumbling of the wheels of a farm cart hurl us all into eternity. Not merely ourselves and our children, our fine vines, our homes and our national forest, but also the Swiss, the French, the Dutch, the Germans, the Italians, and the Spanish. Indeed, the whole of Europe, which is the cradle of Western civilization. The man Bascomb should be impeached and exiled. He has achieved a victory quite contrary to the wishes of his government. You will recall, your Grace, that it was our plan to lose this war. Contrary to this plan, indeed, almost in defiance of it, Bascomb has won it."

Gloriana smiled a little smile of satisfaction. She was thrilled at Tully's unparalleled success, and admired him as she had no other man, including her father. Her reaction, however, was lost on the Count of Mountjoy who stormed on.

"What are we to do now?" he demanded. "Rehabilitate the United States, perhaps, as we had anticipated that they would rehabilitate us? That is beyond our capacity were we a people a thousand times our size with a million years in which to achieve the task.

"Who in America will buy the wines of Grand Fenwick after the outrage this villain Bascomb has perpetrated upon that great and innocent people? I repeat, we dispatched him to lose a war and he has impertinently and disastrously won it. Your Grace will recall that in a private audience with his lieutenants, you counseled them to oppose his plan for the secret infiltration of the United States and an attack upon the White House. Instead, he was to attack New York boldly, the object being that he would be immediately defeated and the rehabilitation of Grand Fenwick, according to the traditions of America, would commence upon the morrow.

"Your Grace, there is every precedent for the discharge, if not the impeachment, of those generals and captains who, contrary to the wishes of the executive, vigorously prosecute a war which wiser heads believe should be won by other methods. Far from advancing the prosperity and the security of the duchy of Grand Fenwick, Bascomb has placed us all at the mercy of a foul box containing all the frightful forces of the pit of hell itself."

"Bobo," said Gloriana, "You have been reading Churchill's memoirs and they have had a marked effect upon your oratory. I think it is very nice. But I don't believe we should impeach Mr. Bascomb. I think we ought to have a Privy Council meeting and we ought to ask Dr. Kokintz and Mr. Bascomb to attend. I know it is unusual to have a prisoner of war present at a council meeting of the nation which captured him. But this whole situation is unusual and we need his advice on what this bomb can do and how we can stop it from going off when we don't want it to."

"Whatever your Grace wishes," said the Count of Mountjoy stiffly. "I seek only to serve."

"Don't be angry, Bobo," cajoled Gloriana with one of her little personal smiles. "I really believe that Tully has done something tremendous, only we're not quite sure how to put it to the best use. He is an interesting man . . . indeed a magnificent man. And if you're worried about the bomb going off because of the noise of the carts, give instructions for all the roads past the castle to be covered with straw. That will deaden the vibration."

Tully's return, two months to the day from the time his little force had caught the bus to Marseilles to launch its attack upon the United States, had embodied in miniature all the aspects and details of the victory march of far greater armies of far greater countries through the centuries. The brig *Endeavor,* slipping out of New York harbor had headed north to catch the prevailing westerlies off the Canadian coast. The Atlantic crossing had been achieved in ten days. Favorable winds and the Portuguese current had brought the *Endeavor* swiftly to the Gibraltar straits, and the worst part of the voyage had been the three days consumed in getting to Marseilles with the uncertain Mediterranean breezes blowing from every quarter. From there, the Fenwickians had taken the bus to the borders of the duchy and then disembarked. Tully held them two hours at the border while mail and bows were polished, all made as splendid as might be, and the duchess notified of the return of her army. Then with a fanfare on hunting horns, with the banner of Grand Fenwick held proudly aloft, the little force crossed the border into its homeland.

Every man, woman, and child in Grand Fenwick was there to welcome the returning soldiers. They cheered, they wept, they sang, they embraced each other and they embraced the longbowmen. They strewed the road before the warriors with flowers and they hung garlands around their necks. And when the body of Tom Cobley, representing the casualties of the campaign, was carried by, they bowed their heads and prayed for him.

The order of the march was as follows. First came Tully clad in his mail and surcoat, with Will at his side carrying the Grand Fenwick banner. Immediately behind, bewildered and nervous, were Dr. Kokintz, General Snippett, and the four New York policemen, closely guarded by ten bowmen and two other men at arms. Behind them was Stars and Stripes at half-mast to signify the defeat of the United States. Then, on a plank, held shoulder high by two men, and cushioned with straw, was the Q-bomb. Bringing up the rear, and draped with the Fenwick banner, was the body of Tom Cobley. All of war was there—the triumph, the captives, the prize and the dead. Tully led his men to the courtyard of the castle where the duchess awaited their arrival, and here the ceremony officially announcing the victorious conclusion of the campaign was enacted.

The duchess stood upon the castle steps, flanked by the Count of Mountjoy, representing the Anti-Dilutionists, and Mr. David Benter, representing the Dilutionists. As a special honor, Tully's father, Pierce Bascomb, stood with them to the right of Mountjoy. When the men were assembled in the courtyard, Will saluted Gloriana by bringing the banner down so that the head of the staff touched the ground before her, and raising it again. Tully went down on one knee and asked leave to report that he had successfully attacked the United States, taken six prisoners and captured the greatest weapon in the whole of the American arsenal.

Gloriana had considerable difficulty in controlling herself on hearing this news—a difficulty exceeded only by that of the Count of Mountjoy, who, to his credit, this being a public occasion, managed to keep his monocle in place though only by putting his hand swiftly to it. Both had expected news through the nearby American Consulate that the whole army had been captured and interned. Their only secret worry had been whether the United States would refuse to recognize that a state of war existed between the two countries and bill Grand Fenwick for the board, keep, and repatriation cost of its expeditionary force. That would indeed have been disastrous. To discover that far from this being the case, the army was back of its own accord, victorious, with prisoners and had captured also, if Tully was to be believed, America's most powerful weapon was next to incredible.

"What weapon is this?" Gloriana asked in a carefully modulated voice.

"A bomb, your Grace, which can destroy the whole of Europe," said Tully. He rose to his feet and beckoned the soldiers who carried the Q-bomb on the plank. They brought it before Gloriana, who looked at the little box in disbelief and was about to pick it up.

"*No! No!*" shouted Dr. Kokintz. "Don't touch it. It will destroy everything."

"Silence," roared Tully, "and don't faint on parade." And then to Gloriana: "What he has to say, your Grace, is true. He is the man who made this bomb though he is as weak as a mouse himself. It is the only bomb of its kind in the world, and if he is to be believed, it will, on exploding, wipe out an area of two million square miles."

There was a whisper around the courtyard among the people who had managed to crowd into it to view the ceremony, and they crouched back against the walls to be as far away from the little box as possible. Mothers held their children more closely and husbands pushed their wives behind them. All looked at the bomb on the plank and when the whispers died down there was only silence. The sun seemed for a moment to have lost its warmth and the castle looked old and weary beyond words.

"Take it inside," Gloriana commanded almost in a whisper. "And put it in the deep dungeon. It must not hurt our people."

Tully bowed. "By your leave," he said, "it will never hurt any people."

The bomb was carried into the castle to be placed under guard in the deep dungeon, and the ceremony continued. Tully surrendered his prisoners to Gloriana, and spoke of the bravery of the man who had fallen during the war. "He spoke no word, your Grace, when he died," he said, "but when he was struck down, he rose again to fight with what little of life there was left in him."

"Had he any family?" Gloriana asked.

"None," replied Tully.

"But he was brother to us all," said Gloriana, "and all of us his kin. He was of the common sort, yet more noble in his death than many who claim better blood are during their whole lives. He shall be laid to rest beside Sir Roger Fenwick, and the day of his death will be known as Cobley Day, so that the sacrifice he made for his nation will be remembered as long as his nation survives."

The ceremony concluded with an address by Gloriana in which she paid tribute personally to Tully and generally to all who had accompanied him on the expedition. She capped it by announcing, to thunderous cheers which made Dr. Kokintz very nervous for the Q-bomb, that a feast would be held in the grand banqueting hall of the castle to which all were invited. Then she took Tully aside and requested him to wait on her in the private-audience chamber.

When they were alone Gloriana did not know precisely what to say. It aggravated her that this was the one man in the whole duchy in whose presence she was always at a loss on how to begin. She seated herself at a circular table and beckoned him to a chair opposite. He was, she noted, very bronzed and somehow seemed bigger and more male than he had before. When she looked at him, she felt a sort of lightness. Her heart seemed to beat faster and her voice was a little hard to control.

Tully looked at the fair hair like a cap of gold, the proud chin, the firm eyes, and then turned quickly to examine his hands placed on the table before him.

"Tell me all your story," Gloriana said, "and tell me particularly about this bomb."

Tully did so, omitting no details and adding such facts as he had learned about the bomb from Dr. Kokintz during the return voyage.

"What are we to do with it?" Gloriana asked when he was finished.

"The first thing which we must do," said Tully, "is to guard our frontiers day and night. The Americans will try to get it back. Others may also try to steal it, for who has this bomb has mastery over all the nations because of the threat the bomb represents. Both sides, the Americans and the Russians, may send agents to get the bomb. But we are fortunate in two respects. Our frontiers are easily patrolled and aliens can be readily excluded. And if one should manage to get past the border, he would be quickly recognized because, being as small as we are, everyone in Grand Fenwick knows the other by sight. A stranger would soon be discovered.

"The Americans or the Russians might try to drop someone here by parachute. But again, because we all know each other so well, a parachutist even if dropped at nighttime would not have much chance. Side by side with guarding our borders a guard must be placed around the castle to prevent anyone entering who has no official business. And a double guard must be put on the dungeon where the bomb is. That guard must be maintained twenty-four hours a day; and must be instructed to admit no one to the dungeon but yourself."

"I am worried about this," Gloriana said frankly. "We may have made ourselves the most powerful nation in the world, as you say, but that's not what we wanted to do at all. What we went to war for was just to get enough money by honorable means to be able to continue free as we have always been. All we get for being the most powerful nation in the world is that we have to live in a stage of siege, with our frontiers patrolled, everybody eying his neighbor with suspicion, and all afraid of being exterminated at any moment if that beastly bomb explodes. We're a lot less free now than we were before, and I can't say that I like it."

"Victory sometimes carries more responsibilities than gains," replied Tully. "That is because it marks the return of conscience. In time of war, conscience is put aisde, and it used to be kept aside, at least in so far as the conquered were concerned. It used to be a case of the spoils for the victors and woe for the conquered. War had some sense then. But nowadays we suffer from the mistake of being half civilized. We turn barbarian during war as a matter of patriotism, and civilized when the war is over as a matter of humanitarianism. We first kill off as many of the enemy as we can by as efficient a method as we can devise, and then save as many of them as we are able with all the energy and wealth at our disposal. War, in fact, has become an atrocious waste of time. Unconditional surrender brings as its corollary unrestricted rehabilitation. If it were possible to devise a method whereby each side could half win a war and no more, things, of course, would be different; but, then, that cannot be done."

Gloriana did not follow this very clearly. She was of a practical rather than theoretical nature and Tully's talk of the responsibilities of victory disturbed her.

"I hope you're not leading up to telling me that we'll have to rehabilitate the United States," she said, "because if so, we'll have to borrow the money from them to do it."

Tully laughed.

"No," he replied. "We of Grand Fenwick have achieved the military miracle of the twentieth century—a war in which the victor doesn't have to give a penny to be vanquished. But we don't get off quite free. Before we went to war, our responsibility was to ourselves alone. Now our responsibility extends to all mankind. We must keep the bomb out of the hands of those who might use it, because in the kind of warfare in which such a weapon would be employed all humanity, not just individual nations, is likely to be exterminated.

"It is not easy, I know, to be thrust into the role of world custodian in so short a time, after being as small a nation as we were. Much bigger nations have found the burden very heavy. The United States itself after World War II suddenly found that it had become the premier nation of the world, and was at a loss what to do about it. Many did not want to be the premier nation at all, but would have preferred to go back to the way they were. But that was impossible for them then, as it is for us now."

"If the Americans offer us millions and millions of dollars for the bomb, don't you think we ought to give it back to them?" Gloriana asked.

Tully stood up and braced his shoulders. He put his hand on the hilt of his broadsword and Gloriana was reminded once again of his odd likeness to the portrait of Sir Roger Fenwick.

"We are charged," he said solemnly, "by the very possession of this bomb with the duty of bringing the world back to sanity. You, your Grace, are no longer merely the ruler of the duchy of Grand Fenwick. You are the most powerful woman in the world. The lives of millions hang upon your word. You have but to give me the command, and I will explode that bomb with one blow from my mace and destroy the whole of Europe. With such power, all nations are compelled to treat with you. Far-reaching agreements for world peace, effective because they can be enforced by the threat to detonate this bomb, can be achieved. Your ancestors never failed their nation. You are called upon now not to fail the whole world."

"But surely other nations will in time be able to make such a bomb as this," Gloriana said.

"True," replied Tully, "and it is to the problem of preventing them that we must apply ourselves. I would suggest that you call a meeting of the Privy Council to examine the matter in all its aspects."

It was after the private audience with Tully that the Count of Mountjoy urged that he be impeached and exiled for bringing the bomb into Grand Fenwick. When Gloriana had brushed aside his suggestion, the Privy Council meeting was summoned for the following day.

15

THE MEETING OF THE PRIVY COUNCIL OF THE DUCHY OF Grand Fenwick coincided to the day with a meeting of the Cabinet of the United States in the office of the President, and a meeting of the Presidium of the Soviet Union in the Kremlin. The topic on the agenda of all three meetings was the same—the Q-bomb.

Because of the difference in local times, the meeting of the Presidium was held first. It was a brief session and could hardly be called a meeting, in the sense of a convention for an exchange of views, so much as an address by one person to a number of others who were called upon to listen to it. A heavy-jowled man in a uniform so devoid of decorations as to be almost monastic sat at the head of a long mahogany table with a sheet of paper before him. Perhaps a dozen others lined the two sides of the table. They bore a remarkable likeness to each other of which the similarity of their clothing was merely the reflection. Their faces had the same set look. Their eyes had the same unrevealing stare. Their mouths were set in the same straight line and their hands were all placed upon the table top as if this was some kind of a drill.

The man at the head of the table looked them over seeking, as it were, to uncover any departure from the overall uniformity—a handkerchief in a breast pocket, perhaps, or a mechanical pencil. Satisfied that no such deviation had been perpetrated, he commenced to read in a curiously high-pitched voice, quite at odds with his appearance.

"The proletariat of the independent state known as the duchy of Grand Fenwick," he piped, "subjected to intolerable economic warfare by the capitalist imperialists of Wall Street, have united with the workers of the world to throw off the bonds of serfdom imposed upon them by these bestial exploiters of humanity.

"The proletariat of the duchy of Grand Fenwick, placing themselves in the vanguard of the proletariat everywhere which seeks to escape the chains of the capitalist masters, have declared war upon the United States of America. Hurling themselves like the heroes of our own glorious revolution against the fortresses of the economic royalists, they have invaded the city of New York, and with losses amounting to twenty-five per cent of their total force, seized the Q-bomb with which the barbarous money worshipers sought to destroy the whole civilized world.

"This Q-bomb is one which we, as a civilized people, refrained from making ourselves although it was well within the skill of our comrade scientists.

"It is proposed therefore that the people of the Union of Soviet Socialist Republics join forces with the heroic proletariat of the duchy of Grand Fenwick to protect them from reprisals from the capitalist imperialists and see that the Q-bomb is secured from falling into the hands of the enemies of the people.

"It is proposed that the Commissar of Foreign Affairs visit the chief of the proletariat of the Grand Fenwick who is a woman called Gloriana and offer her on behalf of the Soviet Union ten divisions of the Red Army for the protection of the people and the Q-bomb. He will propose that the Q-bomb be taken to Moscow for safekeeping and a treaty of eternal friendship and mutual protection be concluded between the place called Grand Fenwick and the Union of Soviet Socialist Republics.

"Vote."

Twelve hands around the table shot up. The heavy-jowled man nodded, picked up his papers and they all filed out of the room.

The meeting of the Cabinet of the United States was equally as serious though by no means as formal. The President wore a lightweight suit of a new synthetic material, for the late spring in Washington was unmercifully hot. The Secretary of Defense was more formally attired in a suit of blue serge. He wore a polka-dot tie, which by its neatness and its smallness increased his marked likeness to a mouse. The Secretary of State leaned to formality too, though he permitted himself a suit of Oxford gray and a club tie of narrow black and white stripes.

Senator Griffin, who as chairman of the Atomic Energy Commission had also been invited to attend, wore his unvarying uniform of light gray with a small rosebud in his lapel. His red choleric face showed signs of great strain. The Secretaries of the Treasury and Agriculture were not present nor the Secretary of the Interior. But their places were taken by an admiral, a five-star general of the army, and an air force general. The army general wore a battle jacket with a pale-blue ribbon of the Congressional Medal on it and a pair of GI pants were tucked into cowboy boots. He had paid $250 for the cowboy boots, which were handmade. He came from Texas and had a reputation for being a man of action, impatient of what he called "palaver."

"I suppose," said the President, "that you have all seen this." He held up a copy of the *New York Daily News*. The headline read NEW YORK INVADED. Below was the line Q-BOMB CAPTURED BY ENEMY. And below that SCIENTIST MISSING.

"Saw it," said the army general. "Didn't pay it much attention. Other day they had a story about New York being invaded by some jerks from Mars. Lot of baloney."

"Unfortunately," said the President gravely, "it isn't. New York was invaded during the alert by a small group of raiders from the duchy of Grand Fenwick. They did capture the Q-bomb. And they also captured Dr. Kokintz, the only physicist in the world who knows how to make this bomb. And they got away clean in a sailing vessel and now have the bomb and Dr. Kokintz. They have, in fact, the power to destroy the whole of Europe. And if they got the bomb over here, the power to destroy most of the United States. The point is: What are we going to do about it? I should like an expression of views from you gentlemen."

The members of the Cabinet looked at each other like boys in a classroom who had been asked quite a simple question but were unable to come up with the answer. The silence continued until it was almost painful. The Secretary of Defense sought comfort in placing his fingers to his mouth. Senator Griffin glared at the floor between his feet as if at any moment he would launch into a full-dress denunciation of the carpet. The Secretary of State crossed his legs and played a little tattoo with his fingers on a portfolio on his knees. The army general was the first to speak.

"Heck, Mr. President," he said. "I don't know what all the backing and filling's about. Give me forty parachutists and a plane and I'll go over to that little jerkwater country and get that bomb and this Kokintz back before they know what's happened to them."

The President smiled. "That would mean an overt attack on the duchy of Grand Fenwick," he said.

"We aren't scared of them, are we?" the general asked, surprised.

"No," said the President. "But it isn't that simple. Technically we are at war with the duchy, so we would be within our rights to mount any kind of attack we desire against the country. But there's world opinion to be considered. We cannot let it be recorded in history that a nation of our size attacked the smallest country in the world—a state which is only five miles long and three miles wide, and cherishes the same love of freedom that gave us birth. We cannot do that, whatever the provocation. It would be contrary to all the traditions of our country. I do not believe for a moment that our own people would stand for it. And it would completely wreck our relations with the smaller foreign nations, especially the South American republics whose friendship and trust is essential to our own security. They would see in such an attack the iron fist in the velvet glove. That is one point.

"There is another point too. Putting aside these moral

and diplomatic considerations which must weigh very heavily, the people of Grand Fenwick have given us ample proof of their patriotism and their sense of independence. It is not beyond the bounds of possibility that if they were invaded by us and overwhelmed, they would elect to destroy themselves and the whole of Europe rather than submit to defeat. When Patrick Henry said, 'Give me liberty or give me death,' he spoke not only for the early Americans but voiced the secret creed of millions of people living in a hundred different countries throughout the world. He spoke not only for his time but for our time too. We cannot run a risk of the physical disintegration of Europe, which in the long run would certainly be blamed on us, even to regain the possession of the Q-bomb."

He paused for a while and then said, each word spoken deliberately and grimly, "What we have to realize is that with the seizure of the Q-bomb and Dr. Kokintz, Grand Fenwick has achieved a victory which it is impossible for us to reverse. The center of the world's military power has shifted from this continent to that tiny nation. This is a hard thing for us to grasp, but it is nonetheless true."

"Is it not possible to get the bomb back by the use of secret agents?" the Secretary of Defense asked.

"I've gone into that," the President replied. "I have discussed with the Office of Strategic Services the possibility of some of their skilled men dropping into Grand Fenwick from a plane or getting there by other means to recapture the bomb and Kokintz.

"The OSS is of course willing and anxious to try. But they make no attempt to belittle the difficulties. I hardly have to point out that a stranger in so small a country would be immediately noticed and arrested. The borders are, of course, completely guarded. The bomb, according to information received by our agents, is kept in the dungeon of a castle. The castle is closely guarded. The dungeon is under a double guard. The whole place is completely sealed against entry. But, even supposing that one or more of our agents did get into the country unnoticed, they would have to kill or incapacitate the guards to get to the dungeon where the bomb is kept. Then they would have to escape through an aroused country with a weapon which if dropped or bumped would kill millions and leave as an aftermath a gas which would kill millions more—an extremely stable gas which once it is formed would take its toll of lives for decades, none knowing which nation or community would next be visited. The risk of the bomb being exploded while being taken from Grand Fenwick is more than we dare expose the world to. We must find some other way out of this quandary."

"Mr. President," said the Secretary of Defense, "there is one other important aspect of this problem which we must not overlook. It is well enough to say that we cannot go down in history as having attacked the smallest nation in the world. It is well enough to point to the dangers surrounding an attempt to seize the bomb by use of secret agents. But no such scruples will deter the Communists.

"We agreed when we were discussing the manufacture of the bomb with Dr. Kokintz that it would give world mastery, temporarily at least, to whoever possessed it first. The same argument holds true now. We must not ignore the probability that the Russians themselves may invade Grand Fenwick and, risking the consequences, seize the Q-bomb. Or they may use secret agents to get it. If they should succeed, they could force whatever terms they wished upon us under threat of using the bomb against us.

"They could demand our complete withdrawal from Europe, for instance. They could demand cessation of all aid to nations combating Communism; the handing over of the people and territory of Western Germany to their control; admission of Red China to the United Nations; the removal of all barriers to the free operation and organization of the Communist party in the United States."

He stopped and shrugged and made a gesture of helplessness with his hands. "In fact," he continued, "there is no limit to what we would have to agree to in order to save as much as we could of our nation and our people. They could dictate the whole order of the world. Useless to say that the Kremlin would not do these things. World conquest is their averred goal, and to attain their objectives, the Communists have slaughtered thousands of their own people without a qualm. They are ruthless in a sense and to a degree which it is hard for us to grasp even when the evidence is laid plainly before us. Our primary problem, as I see it, is not so much to regain possession of the Q-bomb as to prevent Moscow from getting hold of it. And that could mean war."

"Pretty tough fighters, those Russians," said the army general, half to himself. "They made a hell of a stand at Stalingrad. Take lots of tanks and artillery to get through them. Congress ought never to have cut back the army estimates. I had a hunch something like this was going to happen."

"Heavy bombers would be more important than tanks," said the air force general.

"Unnecessary if we had plenty of carriers to attack through the Baltic and the eastern reaches of the Mediterranean," interposed the admiral.

The three glared at each other.

"Gentlemen," said the President patiently. "We have not gone to war yet. Despite recent precedents, a declaration of war by the United States still requires the consent of the Congress."

The Secretary of State uncrossed his legs. The action had become known in international diplomatic circles as a signal that he had something to say. Its significance was well understood by the Cabinet and all gave him their attention.

"I received this morning a short coded message from our ambassador to the Kremlin which there was just time to decipher before attending the present meeting," he said. His voice was as conservative, as lacking in sparkle and luster as his club tie. "The message has some bearing on the Kremlin's intentions in the matter."

He opened his portfolio precisely and took out a piece of thin blue paper. "Here is the message," he said. "Confidential, of course." And he gave a quick glance in the direction of Senator Griffin.

> Presidium voted this morning to offer ten divisions of the Red Army for the protection of Grand Fenwick against U.S. attack. Foreign commissar leaving to negotiate mutual assistance and protection pact and try to get Q-bomb to Moscow for safekeeping. Details follow with pouch. Hancock.

"Who's Pouch?" asked the army general.

"Diplomatic pouch," said the secretary with a slight smile. "Not a person."

"Read that again," the President interrupted, a little testily. The Secretary of State did so.

"What do you make of it? Do you think this means that they are going to invade?" the President asked.

"It's always difficult to discover precisely what the Russians mean," the secretary parried. "Particularly so when all we have to form a judgment on is a short message transmitted in code. Hancock is scrupulous, however, about the selection of the precise wording for such messages. I believe we will not be far wrong if we interpret this 'offer' as meaning that ten divisions of the Red Army are to be sent to that part of their occupied territory nearest to the Fenwick border ready to invade. That would be Neufelden in Austria, about two hundred miles distant. Call it five hours away for mechanized troops traveling overland and something less than an hour for airborne divisions. We might presume that a large number of the Russian divisions will be airborne. We have sufficient experience of totalitarian methods to realize that an offer of friendship and mutual assistance is usually notice of intention to annex. Similarly, an offer of troops for protection is usually notice of intention to occupy."

Senator Griffin broke the shocked silence which followed.

"We must take immediate and effective countermeasures, Mr. President," he burst out. "We must match the Soviet offer of mutual assistance and friendship with one of our own. We must offset their offer of ten divisions with an offer of twenty, if need be. I have no doubt," he added, "that Congress will give its fullest support to such measures."

"We're overlooking something basic here," said the President. "That is that we are at war with the duchy of Grand Fenwick. We cannot send troops to protect the enemy. Such an offer would be rejected out of hand. Not only are we at war with Grand Fenwick, but at the present stage of the hostilities we have lost, and have arrived at an impasse where we can do nothing further. We must, before we can take any countermeasures against the Russians, sue for terms and arrange a peace."

"You mean that the United States of America with its one hundred and sixty million people, its enormous industry, its incalculable wealth, its massive armaments has to sue for terms from a nation whose total population wouldn't make a good gate at a football game? Preposterous," snorted Senator Griffin.

"Preposterous but true," replied the President. "I don't suppose the British relished it any better when Cornwallis surrendered to us. We were a very small nation then, and they a very big one. Does anybody have an alternative plan?"

Nobody had. It was agreed that the Secretary of State would fly to Grand Fenwick in the Presidential plane with plenipotentiary powers to arrange a peace between the two nations, and back this up by a mutual assistance pact and the offer of fifteen divisions of the United States Army for protection of the duchy against aggression. Senator Griffin was somewhat mollified to learn that the fifteen U. S. divisions could be held in readiness at Linz in the U. S. zone in Austria, only a few miles from where the Soviet divisions were likely to be stationed.

"Promise them anything within reason," the President instructed the Secretary of State. "We'll see that the

San Rafael Pinot, which caused all this, is withdrawn immediately from the market. We'll give them preferential treatment for the importation of their own wine into the United States in any quantity they ask. We'll give them money, machinery, technical assistance—anything. You will, of course, attempt in return to secure agreement for the Q-bomb to be restored to us, and Dr. Kokintz too. But if that is impossible, it is essential to obtain a firm guarantee that it will not be given to the Russians. You'd better get General Snippett and the four policemen back as well," he said almost as an afterthought.

He looked the Secretary of State over with a calculating eye. "I don't want to be personal," he added, "but the ruler of Grand Fenwick is, I understand, a rather attractive young woman. You might bear that in mind and try to look a little more—er—dashing. You'd better take along some presents. What would you suggest?"

The Secretary of State was about to suggest twelve cases of the finest New York champagne, but recollected himself and said, "Perhaps a mink coat?"

"No," snorted the President. "And that goes for deep freezers too. Think of something else."

They settled on a diamond necklace and the secretary was to inquire discreetly into the availability of nylon stockings and lingerie in Grand Fenwick—this because the experience of World War II suggested that such gifts could perform wonders with the female population of Europe.

Midway in time between the meeting of the Presidium and the Cabinet of the United States, the Honorable Byron Partridge rose in the House of Commons in London to ask a question of the Foreign Secretary.

"Is Her Majesty's Government aware," he asked, "of reports that the duchy of Grand Fenwick has declared war upon the United States of America and that an expeditionary force of the duchy is believed to have invaded New York City and seized a bomb known as the quadium bomb, which, according to report, is capable of destroying an enormous area?"

The Foreign Secretary rose slowly, gave a slight bow and said, "Her Majesty's Government is fully acquainted with all the facts of the case." Then he sat down again.

"Is Her Majesty's Government prepared to reveal what steps are being taken, if any, to deal with the problems arising out of this situation?" the Honorable Byron Partridge persisted.

The Foreign Secretary leaned over to whisper in the ear of the Prime Minister, who was seated next to him. The Prime Minister appeared to be asleep. His eyes were closed and, in the silence, honorable members could hear what sounded like a slight snore coming from him. When the Foreign Secretary had finished whispering, however, the Prime Minister was heard to snort like a bulldog and say distinctly, "Your pigeon, Tony."

The Foreign Secretary rose again and surveyed the House slowly, starting with the lower benches opposite him and ending with a glance at the Distinguished Strangers' Gallery, where he had been informed the Russian ambassador was seated, having come to hear the debate.

He put his hands in the pockets of his trousers and swaying slightly on his feet said, "I would call the attention of the honorable member for North Westhampton to the treaty concluded between the duchy of Grand Fenwick and the kingdom of England in the year 1402. Under the provisions of this treaty, Her Majesty's Government is obliged to send full and sufficient assistance—I quote the precise wording—to the duchy of Grand Fenwick should it be threatened by any foreign power whatsoever.

"Her Majesty's Government is satisfied that the present situation calls for the implementation of this clause of the Treaty of 1402, the original of which the honorable member may examine in the Records Office if he so desires. The House, I am sure, will not expect details of troop movements at this time, but I believe it is in order to divulge that eight divisions are involved, four of them

airborne. I shall myself be leaving shortly to assure her
Grace the Duchess Gloriana XII personally of our intention to fulfill the provisions of this ancient and honorable pact in all their implications." The Foreign Secretary sat down.

There was a burst of cheering in which the members
of Her Majesty's Loyal Opposition joined. The Russian
ambassador glared down at the Foreign Secretary, who
was smiling upward in his direction, and rushed out.

In Paris a resolution to send similar aid to the defense
of the duchy was made in the Chamber of Deputies.
But the government collapsed over the issue of overtime
rates for taxi drivers before the motion could be voted
on.

16

IN THE DUCHY OF GRAND FENWICK, THE MEETING OF THE
Privy Council to discuss the Q-bomb was the most extraordinary of all those held, whether in Moscow, in
Washington, in London, or in Paris. For the most important person at the meeting, indeed, the individual
who held the key to its success or its failure, was the
captured American scientist Dr. Kokintz. And he was
placed in the peculiar situation of being called upon to
help his captors secure the full fruits of their victory by
giving them advice about the Q-bomb.

Dr. Kokintz was much perturbed about his situation.
He was seated at one side in the Great Hall of Fenwick
Castle. At a table a little distance away were the members of the Privy Council. There were present Duchess
Gloriana, the Count of Mountjoy, Mr. Benter, Tully Bascomb, as high constable of the Fenwick Army, and by
special invitation his father Pierce Bascomb, invited because he was acknowledged to be the wisest and the
most learned man in the whole duchy. It was not the
presence of his captors that disturbed Dr. Kokintz, nor
the fact that they were dressed in the garb of the fourteenth century. Nor was he upset about the mailed
soldiers, both of them well over six feet, who stood on
either side of him. What caused him his anguish was
the emotional and mental conflict within him between
patriotism and humanitarianism; between Dr. Kokintz,
loyal citizen of the United States, and Dr. Kokintz, foremost scientist of the world, whose training and knowledge he sometimes felt belonged not to one country but
to all, since it involved the fate of all.

The Count of Mountjoy had taken the leading part in
the proceedings. He had pleaded, argued, and de-

manded that the Q-bomb be taken back to the United
States immediately since it represented a constant and
imminent menace to all the people of the duchy. "This
man has brought disaster to our country," he exclaimed,
pointing to Tully. "He has imported a powder keg and
demanded that we all sit upon it. I say, in the presence
of his revered father, that he has in the past raised grave
suspicions of his loyalty to this nation. And I say, equally in his father's presence, that his monstrous seizure of
this infernal machine, and his bringing of it back to
Grand Fenwick is nothing more than a plot to extermi-
nate the country, unless some secret terms of his, not yet
revealed, are met."

"What do you mean by that?" Tully demanded.

"My meaning must be perfectly plain to any who
have made a study of the pedigree of the families of
Grand Fenwick," the count replied suavely. "Your own
pedigree traces back through illegitimate birth to Sir
Roger Fenwick. I find that a statute of the Council of
Freemen of 1385 sets aside all claims to the ducal chair
of Grand Fenwick advanced by one Tully Bascomb,
who is identified as the son, born out of wedlock, of
Sir Roger and a woman Marion Bascomb, who was Sir
Roger's mistress. You cannot pretend to be unaware of
this pedigree."

Gloriana glanced at Tully and realized now the source
of the strange likeness between him and her distinguished ancestor.

"I am not only unaware of it," flared Tully, "but I say
that you lie. And if you are man enough to resent the
statement, the matter may be taken up at your conveni-
ence."

Gloriana intervened before the quarrel could go further. She ordered the Count of Mountjoy to withdraw
his allegation and apologize, and Tully to accept the
apology and set aside his anger. "We have need of the
services of both of you," Gloriana said, "and forbid this
difference between you." So the matter was patched up
for the while.

Mr. Benter, next to voice his opinion, said that he

could not agree with the Count of Mountjoy that the Q-bomb should be restored to the United States. "It is a weapon which, anxious as we are to get rid of, they must be more anxious to regain. If we keep it, we may succeed in obtaining from the United States terms of peace which will assure the prosperity of the nation for years to come. And when all is said and done that is why we went to war with the Americans."

"We need to think bigger than this, your Grace," Tully said by way of reminding her publicly of his previous conversation. "It is not a matter of whether we keep the bomb and Dr. Kokintz, or send them back. We will be no safer if we send them back than if the bomb and its inventor remain guarded here. In fact, we will be less safe. For if ever such bombs as this are used in a war they will surely destroy us, even though we are not involved in the hostilities. By keeping the bomb and Kokintz here, we have a small measure of safety. But what we must devise is a plan to ensure that the bomb is never used, nor any others ever manufactured. And that is something on which one man alone is best qualified to advise." He turned towards Dr. Kokintz.

"This man," he said, "made this bomb. He claims he made it because of a fear that the Russians might make one first. And it is his belief that if the Russians made one they would not hesitate to use it if there was any need. He called this bomb a weapon of peace. Maybe he only said that to salve his conscience. But we can now put him to the test and see whether he is prepared to use his knowledge to prevent the manufacture of such weapons in the future anywhere in the world."

Gloriana turned to Dr. Kokintz. "Do you have anything to say?" she asked.

Dr. Kokintz stood courteously and gave her a slow bow. "What am I to say?" he asked. "If I take part in these proceedings, I will be a traitor to my own country. I am a citizen of the United States with whom you are at war. You are enemies of my country. I can say nothing."

"Dr. Kokintz," said Tully, "you hide behind a sham.

You are supposed to have more intelligence than any man in the world. Yet you pretend you cannot tell the difference between a false position and a true one. You say that you are a citizen of the United States but ignore the fact that you are first a member of the human race. You say that your duty lies to America, but where does your duty to the human race lie? Does your position as a citizen of the United States give you the right to make a weapon which can destroy millions of your fellow beings? Which comes first, your duty to your own kind or your duty to your country?"

"I do not know," Dr. Kokintz replied wearily. "I do not know. All I know is that when they try me, it will not be as a member of the human race but as a citizen of the United States."

"You know, but you will not admit it," said Tully contemptuously. "You are nothing more than an educated serf. You take orders involving the fate of millions which you alone can carry out, and then you try to escape from the consequences of obeying these orders by calling it patriotism."

Dr. Kokintz took off his thick glasses and, his hands clenched by his sides, advanced toward Tully.

"You are a young man," he said, "and so you talk of high principles not from knowledge of them but through ignorance. The problem which confronts me is one with which you will never be confronted. Scientists such as I have become creatures of another world. Our very work deprives us of the normal moral values which guide the layman. No one understands what we do but ourselves. We communicate with each other in a language which can only be understood by ourselves and by no others— the language of nuclear physics. We know better than anyone else the terrible potentialities of our work. Yet we are bound by the laws of other men. We are gods or devils, whichever the others make us. The harm or good which comes from our work is their choice and their doing. It is they who decide whether millions will die or whether they will live such lives as have never been lived before—longer lives, happier lives, lives freer of disease. Do not condemn the scientist, young man. Condemn rather the laymen of all nations who control the scientists; the laymen who cannot agree among themselves and as a result compel us to play the part of destroyer. War existed before science. The crime which is done now is that war has made a tool and slave of science, and man's knowledge, painfully and laboriously compiled, is made the instrument of man's destruction."

In all this time, Pierce Bascomb had been sitting quietly at the council table quite untroubled by the accusations against his son or the impassioned defense by Dr. Kokintz of his position. A bird chirped in the courtyard outside and he cocked his head to listen to it. The bird burst into a melodic cadenza running through a double octave and then ending on two comical little notes as if the whole thing were a joke. Dr. Kokintz listened to it and smiled. He turned to look at the guards on either side of him and noticed that they were smiling too, like pleased children.

"That is one of our Grand Fenwick sparrows," one of them whispered. "In early summer I have been told they sing more bravely than sparrows anywhere else in the world."

Pierce Bascomb rose, now that the tension was broken, and bowing to Gloriana said, "Your Grace, I have a suggestion to make concerning Dr. Kokintz. He has been taken from his own country and brought on a long hard journey to a strange land. He is our prisoner, but this is really nothing new to him, for he has not been a free man for many many years. He has been compelled to work at tasks against which his conscience as a man must frequently have rebelled. He has lived a life of doubt and anxiety with burdens weighing on him heavier than any others, perhaps, have had to shoulder.

"Let us adjourn this meeting for an hour or so, and let Dr. Kokintz come with me not as a prisoner but as a free fellow human being. I would like to take him to our National Forest so that for the first time in many years he can feel again what it is like to be a truly free man, relieved of all restrictions and burdens."

"We must send a guard with him," the Count of Mountjoy said. "He may escape. The forest is not too far from the border. We do not want to be left with this bomb and without the man who can control it."

"I do not believe he will try to escape," Pierce Bascomb said gently.

"Let him give his parole that he will not try," Mountjoy rejoined.

"I do not believe that we should put any restriction upon him," Pierce replied slowly. "We cannot force a man to help us with our problem. If he helps at all, it must be the result of his own free desire to do so. It must be because he recognizes a higher duty than that which he owes to his own nation. And he must discover this for himself. But he cannot discover it while he is our prisoner, or while he is tied by loyalties and patriotism to the service of his own nation. Let him, for an hour or so, be just a man without any ties or pressures— a free man, no more and no less."

"Sir," Tully said to his father, "I am not sure that this is a wise proposal. You have not been about the world as much as I. There is a lot in every man that is deceitful and selfish and treacherous. I do not believe that we can trust this scientist. He will try to escape, and you could not prevent him."

Pierce looked at his son with mild reproof. "It is true that there is a great deal in man that is deceitful," he said. "But the deepest force in any man is toward good. It is for that reason that the murderer will help a child across a fence, and the soldier secretly visit the cemeteries of his enemy. When a man denies the goodness in himself, that is when he really suffers. I believe Dr. Kokintz has been made to suffer a great deal in this way. There is good in him, but it has never had an opportunity of asserting itself. I believe it is time he was given a chance to review his work, and without pressure from one side or another let his conscience decide whether he should continue to make more of these bombs or lend his training to prevent any more being made."

Dr. Kokintz rose slowly and said to Gloriana, "I would like to go to the forest for a while."

"You may go," Gloriana replied softly, "and if you wish to leave Grand Fenwick, you may do so. No one will try to stop you. The meeting will reconvene in an hour and we would like you to be with us to help us. But the choice is yours."

Dr. Kokintz and Pierce Bascomb walked slowly out of the council chamber together. The two men at arms were about to follow but Gloriana signaled them to stay.

"Let him be free," she said. "Even if it is only for a little while."

17

THE FOREST OF GRAND FENWICK, AT THIS TIME, LAY IN
all the loveliness of early summer. The bracken was so
thick and tall that in places it covered the path so that
Dr. Kokintz and Pierce were compelled to tread upon
it, and the broken fronds filled the air with the sweet
smell of growth. The rhododendrons were in full bloom,
forming heaping mounds of red at the base of the trees,
some indeed growing so high that the rich blossoms
made domes of flowers against the sky. Pine trees stood
about like cathedral columns through which bright walls
of sunlight slipped, and at times the two men had to
bend low to get under the branches of spreading oaks;
branches which had the appearance of a quiet strength
under their growths of velvet moss.

There were innumerable voices to be heard, of birds,
of insects, of moving leaves and twigs, of falling water
and of squirrels, chattering between filling the pouches
of their cheeks with sweet young hazel nuts.

Pierce Bascomb led the way up a slight hill and then
down another. In a little dell at the bottom was a fallen
tree and nearby a waterfall, no more than twenty feet or
so high. Here a crystal liquid arc bridged the air to spill
into a quiet pool below. At the edge of the pool were a
few rocks and to one side some water plants over which
a brilliant blue dragonfly with a scarlet head flashed and
hovered.

They sat on a tree trunk and listened for a while to
the splashing of the water into the pool.

"This is our only waterfall—a cherished possession,"
Pierce said at length. "I have made an examination of
the rocks and estimate that five hundred years ago, it
was a foot higher. On that basis we will have a waterfall
in Grand Fenwick for five thousand years, though at

the end of that time it will be only ten feet high. But it gives me a sense of great satisfaction to know that the waterfall will be here centuries after I and all my contemporaries are long forgotten. There is a kind of link with posterity to know that others will have the same pleasure from the waterfall as I. In a way I can live part of their lives and they part of mine. That is, of course, presuming that the world will still be here fifty centuries from now, and there will be life on it."

Dr. Kokintz did not rise to the bait. "The land here must be very fertile," he said. "Things grow in great profusion."

"As long as we have been a nation, this has been a forest," Pierce replied. "Our ancestors walked in these same woods five centuries ago and were shaded in these same woods which still stand around us. Originally, the forest was set aside to provide wood for building, for bows and arrows and for charcoal. There are still a few yews standing from which bows were made four centuries ago. In the course of time, the forest became denuded. But for the past two hundred years it has been forbidden to cut down any of the trees. My son, you know, is the chief ranger, and I his assistant. Sometimes we find it advisable to hew down an old tree which is interfering with the growth of younger ones, or is in danger of falling and destroying others around it. But whenever such an occasion arises, a meeting of the Council of Freemen is held, and a vote taken as to whether the tree shall be cut or not. Almost all the people in Grand Fenwick attend these meetings, because they know each tree in the forest. They have a deep sense of responsibility towards them."

"What is done with the lumber when a tree is felled?"

"The smaller branches are made into charcoal. The heavier wood is used for repairing houses and, perhaps, building new ones. No charge is made for the wood. You would be surprised if you went into one of our homes, how the owner could identify every piece of timber in it, and tell you what tree it came from and where the tree had grown and how it came to be cut down and how old it was at the time. Even after the trees are felled, they still serve the people, sheltering them from the wind and keeping them warm. There is a feeling in Grand Fenwick about our trees as if they were living people."

"I haven't a great deal of patience with such sentiments," Dr. Kokintz said. "Trees are trees. They are not people. They are alive, to be sure, but theirs is a lower form of life. Trees cannot feel anything. It is mere superstition to waste affection on them."

Pierce did not reply directly to this. "I have noticed," he said, "that when we cut down a tree a host of small branches burst out of the stump which is left. The life force in the tree insists upon continuing. Even mutilated and deformed, the tree strives to live on. Would you say that the tree had no feeling?"

Dr. Kokintz shrugged. He had not thought of the matter before. "It proves only that there is still life in the tree stump; that it is not yet dead," he said.

"It proves also, surely, that it wants to continue to live," said Pierce. "All things which have life seek to preserve it and because of this, one is always in doubt whether he has the right to destroy life when he cannot create it. When we fell a tree, my son and I, we know that we destroy not only the tree but also its associations with the past, all the pleasures which it might give, if allowed to live, in the future. That is a great deal. It is not an easy matter to cut a tree down. Because of this, I understood well enough what you meant when you said that scientists are compelled to play the role of god or devil by laymen to whose laws they are subject. I and my son must play god or devil to the trees, felling them or doctoring them according to what the people decide. The trees have no say in the matter; no right of appeal. Yet it sometimes seems to me that they should have."

He picked up a chip of wood, threw it into the pool and watched it swirl around and then drift over to the bank.

"There is one difference between us, however," he continued. "The scientist's power of life and death is over his fellow human beings as well as over what you call the lower orders. Ours is only over plant life. The scientist's work, when turned to war, enables one group of people to obtain the mastery over another. That is well enough, I suppose. But now the stage has been reached where not only the countries engaged in a war must go through its agonies, but also all the other countries who have no part in the war at all and all of nature as well. Like the trees, these other countries are condemned to death without any right of appeal.

"They are condemned not only to death but to obliteration though they have no place in the quarrel. They neither start such wars nor end them. Their fate is only to suffer in the struggles of the giants. They are helpless to save themselves. With such weapons as this bomb of yours, war cannot be limited any longer. It must ruin all. And since it must ruin all, the responsibility of the scientist is extended from his own nation to the whole human race."

"This is the same squirrel cage in which I have been running for the last ten years," said Dr. Kokintz bitterly. "If we did not make the bomb, the Russians would make it. The Russians would make it and we believe would use it. We make it in the hope that we will never use it. It is madness, but how are we to get back to sanity? It is, as I said, not the scientists who must lead the way back to sanity, but the people who control the scientists, and they are so filled with distrust of each other's intentions that an agreement even to ban so outdated a weapon as the atom bomb cannot be achieved.

"There is fear and suspicion everywhere. The Communists fear, by the very nature of their own political philosophy, the capitalists. The capitalists see in Communism the ruination of their way of life. The Asiatics, exploited for centuries, distrust the Europeans. The Europeans, fearful of the enormous populations of Asia and the growth of nationalism and technology in India, in Africa and even in China, fear the Asiatics.

"There is no trust anywhere, and the only safety for a

people lies in having weapons of such terrible power that none dare attack them."

"And where do the little nations fit in in all of this?" Pierce asked quietly.

Dr. Kokintz shrugged. "I do not know," he said.

"You do not know because you do not care about the little nations," Pierce said. "You think that the people who live in them are peculiar and quaint and behind the times and not really important. You forget that they are your fellow beings. You think of them as being a kind of substrata of the human race, of no importance because they have no weight to make felt."

"I suppose that is so," Dr. Kokintz replied. "Whoever has the most weight in the world receives the most consideration. That is the one international law which is recognized by all. You must admit that it would be more disastrous for all free men if the United States were destroyed than if, say, Belgium or Ireland or Grand Fenwick were destroyed."

"Perhaps. But a Belgian or an Irishman or one of our own people would not agree. And so long as the world can contemplate the destruction of a small nation without any deep pang of regret, so long will it be uncivilized. It is the same in the government of communities —the rights of the weakest and poorest citizen must receive the same support as those of the richest and the most powerful. Otherwise civilization is merely a name and not a real force. But without civilization, no individual is safe, no nation is safe, and in these days even the world itself is not safe."

Dr. Kokintz said nothing. He sat watching the water swirling in the pool, one wave riding over the other only to be overtaken and merged in another bigger and more vigorous than itself.

"Tell me," said Pierce, "if an agreement were achieved to abolish the Q-bomb and the atom bomb and these other weapons of mass destruction would it be possible, by international inspection, to be sure that none were made?"

"Yes. That is if the inspecting scientists were given

free access to the nuclear laboratories and installations of all the nations. As far as the Q-bomb is concerned, I believe I am the only man in the world who knows how to achieve it. Others may soon find out. But no other scientist, to my knowledge, would be able to discover whether it was being manufactured except myself."

"If such a system of control was established would you be willing to organize the inspection of nuclear plants and train others to do the work?"

"I would do it, I believe, provided it was not a betrayal of my own nation," Dr. Kokintz replied.

"But this is a matter of all humanity and all living things—all their past, their present and their future," Pierce persisted. "It is not a question of loyalty to one group or one country, but to all living things everywhere from this time on. It affects the existence not only of man, whose worth may be debatable, but of all life upon the earth. You have a duty to the whole world, not merely to one segment of one species."

"The question is hypothetical," Dr. Kokintz said, shrugging. "No such agreement has been achieved and you and I, sitting here in this forest, cannot bring such an agreement about."

"It is not hypothetical at all," Pierce stated. "For I tell you that there will be such an international agreement and very soon. It will not come from the big nations where rivalries are strong. However much they desire such an agreement, they cannot trust each other. So the little nations must force them to enter into such a compact and see that they abide by it."

Kokintz chuckled. "And how will these mice tame the lions?" he asked, half mockingly.

"The biggest of the lions, the United States, is already caught in a trap where all its strength is of no avail," Pierce replied. "We of Grand Fenwick have the Q-bomb, the only one in the world. We are, therefore, suddenly, an overwhelmingly powerful nation. We have the means to make others do our will. We can without difficulty form a League of Little Nations, countries such as Finland, Belgium, Uruguay, and El Salvador, Ireland, Lichtenstein, San Marino, Portugal, Norway, Sweden, Denmark, Paraguay, Peru, Chile, Mexico, Liberia, Egypt, Panama, Switzerland—all the small independent nations in the world. Such a League can solemnly demand that the big nations agree to cease the manufacture of nuclear weapons of all kinds and permit international inspection of their plants by teams of scientists from the neutral small nations to ensure that the agreement is adhered to. If they do not agree to do this under moral pressure, we can threaten as a last resource to explode the Q-bomb."

"I do not put much faith in the power of moral pressure," Dr. Kokintz said. "And as for using the Q-bomb, you would never dare to do that. If it were exploded, you would yourselves be destroyed either from the bomb or from the liberation of carbon fourteen, or from the winds and eruptions of the earth which I believe will follow the detonation of the bomb."

"Do you think that the tree, doomed to fall anyway, would not as soon fall a little earlier and kill the woodsmen?" asked Pierce quietly. "Unless the Q-bomb is banned effectively, we will all be destroyed anyway in someone else's quarrel and by someone else's weapons. We will have no say in the matter. Not even a warning of the date. This way, at least, we have a chance of bringing the world to its senses or facing destruction which we ourselves will initiate."

"I do not believe you will find a man in Grand Fenwick or any other nation who would explode that bomb," Kokintz said.

"I thought you knew my son better," Pierce replied with a touch of pride. "He would not hesitate to detonate it if told to do so."

"Who would tell him, knowing they would perish themselves?" Kokintz persisted.

Pierce got up and looked down at him mildly. "I would," he said.

For a little while neither spoke. Then Pierce said, "I will leave you now. You may go if you wish. The path past the waterfall leads over our border into France. It is only a matter of a hundred yards. There are guards, but they have been instructed to let you by. Once outside you can return to making your bombs."

When Bascomb had gone, Dr. Kokintz stood up slowly and looked at the log he had been sitting upon. A green shoot was growing out of one end of it, strong and straight and full of vigor. He listened for a second to the tinkling of the waterfall and noticed that the big blue dragonfly had settled on a lily pad and was sunning its wings luxuriously.

He looked at the path which led to the French border, and caught the chatter of a bird high in a tree. A nuthatch, he thought, and then he remembered that in Grand Fenwick it was called a sparrow. Ridiculous to differ so obstinately on established names. He watched the bird for a while, flitting like a jewel between the branches, and reached in his pocket as a matter of habit for some crumbs. There were none. He turned and walked back towards the castle of Grand Fenwick.

18

THE ATTENTION OF THE WHOLE WORLD WAS NOW CEN-
tered upon the duchy of Grand Fenwick, which in all
its history had never achieved such fame. There were
maps showing every feature of the country in almost
every newspaper. Some showed the exact location of the
castle on top of the two-thousand-foot mountain. Others
gave a plan, or what purported to be a plan, of the castle, with a heavy cross in the center to mark the exact
place where the Q-bomb was kept.

FENWICK CASTLE CENTER OF WORLD CON-
TROL, the *New York Daily News* said across the top of
a five-column map of the fortress. There were three
pages of pictures of Grand Fenwick, or, to be more accurate, two pages of pictures of the Duchess Gloriana and
one page equally divided between the duchy and the
statesmen who were on missions to the United States.
The two pages of pictures of the duchess compared her
physical dimensions with the Venus de Milo, Rita Hay-
worth, Queen Elizabeth II and what a professor of clas-
sics at a small Eastern college claimed were the probable
proportions of Helen of Troy. Gloriana was shown in
one drawing—for no photographs were available—with
a glass of Pinot in her hand. The caption said that Pinot
Grand Fenwick was esteemed by connoisseurs as the
wine of beauty and the duchess drank two glasses of it
before breakfast daily. Stocks in New York were exhausted on the following day.

The *New York Times* ran a creditable article on the
history of the duchy since its founding in which, on the
suggestion of the chief of the *Times* Washington Bureau,
a great amount of space was devoted to the virtues of
Pinot Grand Fenwick. The *Sydney Morning Herald* in
Australia compared the independent spirit of the people

150

of Grand Fenwick with that of the Australians and said that the sympathy of the Australian people must be entirely on the side of the little nation. Another article on the same page stressed that if a Q-bomb were exploded in Europe it would not affect Australia due to the isolation of the Continent, and that while the negotiations between the duchy and the Big Three would be watched with closest interest there was no need for panic.

The London *Times* also ran a history of the duchy, and a letter from a retired colonel living in Wales pointing out that the duchy could rightly be called a British colony. The letter was suppressed after the first edition. *Pravda* contented itself with a report of the Red Army divisions which stood ready to aid the heroic proletariat of the state of Grand Fenwick in their struggle against the bestial oppressors of the people.

Meanwhile the foreign secretaries of the Soviet Union, the United States, and Great Britian arrived in three separate cars—there being no airport in which they could land in Grand Fenwick—at the borders of the duchy. They arrived within three hours of each other— the Russian Foreign Commissar first, the British Foreign Secretary next, and the United States Secretary of State last. At the Pass of Pinot, the only part of the border through which an automobile road ran to connect the duchy with the outside world, they found their way barred by a company of bowmen under the command of Tully Bascomb.

The Soviet Commissar pleaded, argued, fumed, and raved but all in Russian and all to no avail. Tully merely shook his head and waved him off. The British Foreign Secretary arrived next to find his way blocked not only by the bowmen but more immediately by the car of the Russian Commissar ahead of him.

"Tell that fellow to get off the road," he instructed his chauffeur. "I'm here on official business."

The chauffeur looked at the Red Star on the license plates of the car ahead and said, "I believe it's the Russians, sir."

"The Russians, eh," said the Foreign Secretary. "Probably broken down. Ask him if he wants a tow to the side." The chauffeur departed only to return and report that he couldn't make head or tail of what was said except that the car ahead wasn't going to move. "All they say is 'night,'" he said.

"*Nyet*, old boy," said the Foreign Secretary. "Means 'no.' Well, I suppose I'll have to walk." He got out as languidly as if he were calling on his tailor and sauntered past the Russian car, raising his hat as he went by, but not glancing inside. When he arrived at the border, he called out to Tully. "You in charge here?" Tully said he was.

"Her Britannic Majesty's Foreign Secretary presents his compliments to her Grace the Duchess Gloriana XII and has the honor to request an audience with her Grace on her Britannic Majesty's business," the Foreign Secretary intoned.

"My orders are to let no one by," Tully said grimly, his hand on the hilt of his broadsword.

"Glad to hear it," replied the Foreign Secretary. "Mind passing on my message to her Grace and seeing whether an audience can be arranged? It's rather important."

Tully hesitated. "Who's in the car ahead of you?" he asked.

"Haven't the foggiest idea," replied the Foreign Secretary innocently. "To tell you the truth, didn't even look inside."

"Are they the Russians?" Tully insisted.

"Probably."

"Why are they here?"

"This isn't my line of business," the Foreign Secretary said, "but probably to protect you." He drew a fingernail delicately and deliberately across his throat.

"Why are you here?" Tully demanded.

"Rather not say right now, old man. Think I really ought to take it up with the duchess."

"Protection too?"

The Foreign Secretary stiffened. "I'll wait here for an hour or so for a reply," he said. "Otherwise her Grace can get a message to me at the Ledermuhl Inn in Friedrich-shafen."

On his way back to his car, he stopped for a moment at the Russian vehicle, leaned through the back window and reached out his hand to the Russian Commissar. "Haven't seen you since Potsdam," he said in Russian. "I was a little worried. Not much about you in the papers recently."

The Foreign Commissar laughed. His laugh was a lusty bellow starting as dramatically and ending as suddenly as a clap of thunder. When it was done, he said briskly, "It seems we must wait. I have a little vodka. Would you care to join me?"

"Brought some sandwiches myself," replied the secretary. "Always a good thing to bring sandwiches on this kind of business. Why not let's sit in my car, it's a little more roomy."

"However," said the commissar, "mine is a little more comfortable."

They compromised by remaining each in his own car, sending the provender to each other by their chauffeurs. The Foreign Secretary secretly poured the vodka onto the road. The Soviet Commissar sniffed the sandwiches and gave them to his man who ate them with some suspicion. Midway through their lunch, the United States Secretary of State arrived. He eyed the two cars ahead anxiously, bounded out of his before it had come to a complete stop, and hurried to where Tully was standing.

"I have come on a mission from the United States of America to the Duchess Gloriana," he said. "I am the United States Secretary of State." He opened a portfolio and took from it a document giving his credentials. Tully read this through slowly.

"Do you come under a flag of truce?" he asked.

"Flag of truce?" questioned the secretary, surprised.

"Our nations are at war," Tully reminded him. "If you've come to parley, my instructions are to admit you under a flag of truce. Otherwise you are to be refused admission, and if you attempt to cross the border, you are to be taken prisoner."

"Okay," said the secretary. "I come under a flag of truce." He fished his handkerchief out of his breast pocket, flicked it open and waved it in the air. The bowmen stood aside to let him pass, and under a guard of two, with Tully leading the way, the secretary marched up the road towards the castle, his handkerchief held over his head in his right hand.

Three hours later he returned. He drove immediately to Munich where he put through a telephone call to the White House from the U. S. Army headquarters there.

"Mr. President," he said when he had obtained his connection and identified himself. "Peace can be arranged, but not on the terms for which we hoped. Grand Fenwick will not return the Q-bomb. Nor will they surrender Kokintz. They have a plan for getting the smaller nations together to form a league, which, using the Q-bomb as a threat, would compel the big nations—ourselves, Russia, Great Britian, Canada, and the rest—to agree to the abolition of such weapons, with a system of international inspection to ensure that the agreement is honored in all countries."

"That's the same plan that we advanced ten years ago," the President replied.

"Not quite," said the Secretary of State. "The inspection would be carried out by the smaller nations with Kokintz directing the inspection teams. They argue that the bigger nations can trust the small states to be impartial where they cannot trust each other."

There was a minute or two of silence.

"I think you can say that we'll go along with that," the President said. "We'll agree with anything that will put an end to this nuclear armament race. What about the Russians? They're always the stumbling block."

"I think the Russians will have to agree also," the Secretary of State replied. "There's a kind of local Bernard Baruch here called Pierce Bascomb. His son Tully was the one who invaded New York and captured Kokintz and the Q-bomb. This Pierce Bascomb says that if the Russians or anyone else doesn't agree, Grand Fenwick will explode the bomb anyway and wipe out the whole of Europe."

"That wouldn't bother Russia," the President said. "They'd wipe out the whole of Europe themselves, if they got a chance."

"The bomb itself might not hurt them," replied the Secretary of State, "but that carbon fourteen gas would. The westerly winds set across Europe towards Russia. Their people would die by the thousands. The crops would be wiped out and their land made sterile. They daren't risk it."

"Do you believe they'd really explode the bomb?" the President asked.

"Mr. President," the secretary countered, "would you have believed that they would invade the United States with twenty longbowmen, landing in Manhattan off a chartered sailing vessel?"

"I see what you mean," the President replied. "Well, subject to Senate confirmation, we'll go along with the inspection gladly. They've got us up a tree anyway. What other terms did they want?"

"Withdrawal of that San Rafael Pinot from the market, acknowledgment that there is no duty on their part to rehabilitate the United States, free access of their own wine to America, and five million dollars indemnity."

"Did you say million or billion?" asked the President.

"M for Mother million," the secretary replied.

"Only five million," the President exclaimed. "Why, that's less than we've spent on the Germans in one city."

"The difference, I suppose, is that the Germans lost but Grand Fenwick won," replied the secretary dryly. "But there's a rider. A fellow called Benter, who is one of their cabinet members, wants to use the money to put up a factory which will manufacture chewing gum with a Pinot Grand Fenwick flavor. They want exclusive marketing rights in the United States, no tariffs, and they believe they can make enough money out of the exports of the gum to take care of all their needs for a long time to come."

The President chuckled. "Go ahead and have the peace treaty drafted," he said. "You can agree in principle subject to the usual ratification. What about troops for protection?"

"They say they don't need any and I didn't press the point."

"Oh. I suppose they'll release General Snippett and the policemen?"

"Yes. Snippett is anxious to get back. He has a plan for a new weapon for Civil Defense workers."

"What is it?"

"The longbow."

In the Ledermuhl Inn at Friedrichshafen, to which they retired, the British Foreign Secretary and the Soviet Foreign Commissar met in the American bar for cocktails.

"I wonder," said the Soviet Commissar when they had drunk one or two toasts, "what our American friend is doing in Grand Fenwick?"

"Haven't the foggiest idea," replied the Foreign Secretary. "Probably selling them chewing gum. Cheerio."

19

THE DELEGATES OF THE TINY TWENTY, AS THEY BECAME known in the world's press, met the following week in the Great Hall of Fenwick Castle. In the interim the British Foreign Secretary had been received by Gloriana and for the first time in a distinguished diplomatic career had come away empty handed and completely out of countenance.

He had been sanguine that Britain's offer to implement the terms of the pact of 1402 by sending eight divisions for the protection of Grand Fenwick would be warmly welcomed by the duchy. Instead, he had been told sweetly but firmly by Gloriana that no assistance was needed; that the duchy felt itself quite capable of handling its own affairs. This setback was followed by a preliminary discussion of the proposal to form a League of Little Nations to enforce outlawing of the Q-bomb, and an informal exchange of views on whether Britain would be prepared to co-operate with such a league.

"I felt," he told the Prime Minister afterwards, "rather like Gulliver when he awoke in Lilliput and found himself pinned to the ground by a thousand ropes as fine as a spider's web. All I could say was that her Majesty's government would support any proposal which would put an end to the disastrous nuclear-armaments race which not only has the world on tenterhooks but has crippled our efforts to recover our position in world trade. It was rather a humiliating experience all together. We should have thought of the plan ourselves."

"Don't let it distress you, Tony," the Prime Minister said. "It's happened before. Every now and then one of the small nations gets the lion by the tail and all we can do is co-operate. It's surprising the things that will change the course of history. Today it's a bottle of wine. A cou-

ple of centuries back it was the ear of a sea captain
called Jenkins. That one embroiled the whole of Europe
and had its echoes in the French and Indian wars in the
American colonies. Then we fought the Ashanti for a
hundred years or so over a golden stool. I'm not sure
whether cigars were involved in the Spanish-American
War, but I shouldn't be at all surprised. Tell me, this
Gloriana, is she attractive?"

"Very much so."

"Unmarried, I understand."

"Yes."

"Ah. Pity we haven't got a prince to spare. That would
solve the whole thing nicely."

"I don't think he'd stand a chance," said the Foreign
Secretary. "From what I could make out of it, Gloriana
seemed to have her eye on someone already."

"Good heavens! Not an American, I hope!" exclaimed
the Prime Minister.

"No. One of her own people. Man called Tully Bascomb. He's the one who led the invasion against the
United States and captured the Q-bomb."

"Good-looking young scoundrel, no doubt?"

"I wouldn't call him good-looking. He is a big raw-
boned fellow. Has a kind of distant resemblance to Abra-
ham Lincoln."

"Well," said the Prime Minister, blowing a cloud of
cigar smoke up to the ceiling. "He's of English descent,
and that's a consolation. Wait until the next time I
see the American President. His wartime predecessor
used to get under my skin a bit at some of those conferences, comparing the American Garand with our Lee-
Enfield. Once he went all the way back through history,
with Stalin roaring his head off, and ended up comparing
the Kentucky rifle with the English musket. Maybe I
ought to send the President a couple of longbows with
instructions for use. Or perhaps not. They'd probably im-
prove on them. I suppose the Americans will support
the proposal for a League of Little Nations outlawing
nuclear weapons and so on?"

"Yes," said the Foreign Secretary. "I was given to understand that they'd already agreed in principle. There's a rather significant editorial in this month's *Atlantic* pointing to a parallel between the proposed League and the position of the forty-eight states in relation to the Federal government. It's becoming an American idea already. The Russians are likely to be the ones to raise serious objection. But I think they'll have to fall in line too."

The Soviet Foreign Commissar didn't get to see Gloriana. He saw Tully who had been delegated to speak for her, for Gloriana pleaded indisposition. Actually, she didn't think she was capable of facing up to the Foreign Commissar and thought Tully would do a better job.

Tully did. Speaking through an interpreter, Tully made it clear, when the preliminary niceties had been exchanged, that the duchy of Grand Fenwick had been an independent nation centuries before the Soviet Union had been dreamed of. He emphasized that having obtained possession of the Q-bomb it was not the duchy's intention to hand it over to anyone. And he added that being destroyed by the Q-bomb would be infinitely preferable to everybody in Grand Fenwick to becoming the vassals or dependents of any other country in the world, though he did not mention any nations by name.

"You cannot take it upon yourself to play with the lives of your people," countered the Foreign Commissar, who was unused to such blunt tactics, and decided they called for bluntness in return.

"Coming from you," said Tully, "that is a very strange statement indeed."

"We offer you friendship and the protection of the Red Army," the Foreign Commissar thundered.

"We don't need friendship and we can protect ourselves," Tully replied.

"We will see that this matter gets to the proletariat of Grand Fenwick," the Foreign Commissar stormed. "We will broadcast our offer by radio twenty-four hours a day so that everyone in the duchy knows that you and the other aristocrats here would condemn them to death rather than keep them free for all time by a pact of eternal friendship with the Union of Soviet Socialist Republics."

"We haven't any proletariat in Grand Fenwick," Tully replied quietly. "And we haven't any radios either."

This put a stop to the exchange for a while. Then Tully took the initiative. "I do not want to send you back empty handed to Moscow," he said. "I have a proposition to make which may well ensure peace for your country and for the world." He outlined the plan for the outlawing of nuclear weapons and a system of international inspection.

"The Soviet Union," the Foreign Commissar said, "has been from the start in the forefront of the movement to outlaw the atomic bomb and all such weapons. But we have insisted that as a first step, all stocks of atomic bombs must be destroyed. To this the Americans have consistently refused to agree because their policy is one of world domination."

"All stocks of bombs will be destroyed," Tully said. "All except the Q-bomb. That will remain here as the trust of the League of Little Nations. It will represent the International Police Force which the United Nations agreed to set up but never did."

The Foreign Commissar laughed. "You expect us to render ourselves powerless so that you can dominate the world," he said.

"We're going to dominate the world all right whether you wish it or not," said Tully, "but in the cause of peace. In fact, we dominate the world at present though you are a little slow in realizing it. If we exploded the Q-bomb now, thousands of people would be dying in Russia in six weeks. And there wouldn't be anything you could do about it. Those who didn't die would wish they were dead for they would be doomed anyway. In the past two weeks Dr. Kokintz has been performing some experiments with the gas which this bomb will liberate. Perhaps you would like to see one of the surviving results."

From behind a curtain in the chamber in which they were sitting, he brought a cage. Inside it there was some sort of moving thing. It had no head, but there was a mouth at one end with furry lips which kept opening and closing. There were six legs and some bare patches in the fur which showed a bright blue skin below.

"What is it?" the Foreign Commissar asked.

"It used to be a mouse," Tully replied quietly. "The amount of carbon fourteen to which it was exposed was in the proportion of one part to one hundred thousand. The amount released by the bomb would produce a much greater concentration in the atmosphere. Chances of survival would be very small. But those who did survive, animal or human, would become some sort of monster such as this."

The Soviet Commissar could not take his eyes off the thing in the cage. He fancied he heard some kind of squawking from it. The muscles of the body moved convulsively, and now and then one of the six feet twitched. "Tell me again the details of the plan for control of these weapons," he said.

Tully did so.

"Do the Americans and British agree to it?" the Foreign Commissar asked.

"Yes."

"The inspection will be by neutral scientists of the smaller nations?"

"Yes."

"How are we to know that they will not pass on to the United States and Britain what they discover in our Soviet laboratories?"

"You will have to take our word for it. It is either that or this." And he pointed to the cage.

The Soviet Commissar rose stiffly. "I shall report to Moscow," he said. He gave one more frightened look at the thing and left.

When he had gone Dr. Kokintz came in, peering from behind his thick glasses. "Did it work?" he asked.

"I think so," Tully replied.

"Good," said Dr. Kokintz. "Then I had better let them out." He reached into the cage and took the thing out, flipped it over on its back and undid a zipper. Three

frightened white mice scampered out, two of them
crawling up his arms to crouch upon his shoulders. The
thing collapsed into a mere sack of fur. "We used to play
this kind of a trick on newcomers when I was a student of
biology," he said. "It is surprising what people will believe when their minds have been prepared to accept it."

It was after these conferences with the ministers of
the Big Three that the Tiny Twenty convened in the
castle of Grand Fenwick. The countries represented
were Lebanon, Israel, Ireland, Denmark, Iceland, Ec-
uador, Guatemala, Switzerland, Turkey, Greece, Lichtenstein, Finland, Portugal, Mexico, Saudi Arabia, Norway, Sweden, Belgium, Panama, and Grand Fenwick.

Because there was no possibility whatever of accommo-
way, Sweden, Belgium, Panama, and Grand Fenwick.
it was agreed that they would all stay at Basel, Switzerland, and the Swiss government proposed, setting the
note for an amicable conference, that they be lodged
and fed at Swiss expense. "Switzerland," the Swiss minister said when he made this offer to the assembly, "will
be honored to be the host to the representatives of so
many of her sister nations of equal size and weight in
world affairs."

The conference lasted only two days. The first day
was taken up with the presentation and checking of
credentials. On the second day, the general meeting being called to order, Gloriana XII was elected chairman,
with the delegate for Panana, vice chairman. The
Turkish representative proposed that a committee to establish an agenda be appointed, but the representative
from Ireland moved an amendment that there be no
committee on agenda or any other kind of a committee.

"The big nations get together at these kinds of conferences," he said in a rich brogue, "and it's as plain as Pad-
dy's pig what they're all going to talk about. But they
have to slice the pig up into bacon, and divide it into
hams, and pickle the feet and tan the hide before they
can get down to the facts. And before they're through
with it everybody's forgotten what they were going to

talk about. Some that were on the ham committee think it's the ham that is the most important part of the animal, and those on the bacon end of it swear that if it wasn't for bacon it wouldn't be any pig at all. And so they all go away without making any decisions.

"But we know what kind of a beast we have before us. We're here to form a League of Little Nations to compel the Big Three or the Big Four or the Big Five or however many bigs they are to stop all their shenanigans and get rid of these bombs that will blow us all to bits at any minute. So I move that we don't form any committee at all, or try slicing the pig up one way and another, but get down to business as we are."

This thoroughly mixed illustration delivered with some heat, led to a little confusion. But the delegate from Israel, who, as a matter of alphabetical accident, was seated next to the Irish minister undertook to explain. And having explained, he seconded the motion and it was carried unanimously.

The delegate from Israel was a rabbi and the Irish minister turned to him in an aside and said. "It's the first time that a Catholic nation has found itself indebted to the Jewish faith."

To which the rabbi replied gently, "There was one other occasion. Christianity, you will recall, originated in Palestine."

They both laughed.

The charter establishing the League of Little Nations was agreed on the same day. It had been prepared in draft in advance, and was, for such a historic document, an almost childishly simple statement, containing six main points.

There was no lengthy preamble. Instead it got immediately down to business.

It read:

> The nations whose delegates have signed this document, subject to confirmation by their constitutional procedures, solemnly commit themselves to the following duties and courses of action:

1. They bind themselves together to enforce a world ban on weapons of mass destruction.

2. To achieve this they will set up, under the initial direction of Frederick Kokintz, a committee of scientists who will inspect atomic and other nuclear installations of all kinds in all countries to ensure that no nuclear weapons are being made.

3. They will compel the nuclear nations and others to cooperate with this inspection under threat of detonating the Q-bomb now in the possession of the duchy of Grand Fenwick.

4. This Q-bomb will be the trust of all the nations who ratify this agreement. They pledge themselves to guard it.

5. They will use all their powers of persuasion, whether moral, diplomatic, economic, or military to bring about a more peaceful world.

6. They will do all this in the solemn realization that unless it is done all are eventually doomed.

Nobody wanted to add anything to this document. Nobody wanted to subtract from it. They signed it with little more than a routine speech or two, and the next day its contents were publicized to the world.

Then the delegates of the Tiny Twenty went home. No date was set for their next meeting. Indeed the hope was expressed that they would never have to meet again. But it was agreed that, as a symbol of their solidarity, every month an honor guard of soldiers from a different nation would take over the job of guarding the frontier of Grand Fenwick with the bowmen of the duchy.

The same week the United States House of Representatives received a bill which would permit inspection by the Tiny Twenty of the nation's atomic installations. Two weeks later the United States, Britain, Canada, and the Union of Soviet Socialist Republics had agreed to dismantle their atomic arsenals. A month later teams of scientists from the Tiny Twenty were inspecting the nuclear installations of the Big Four Powers. The world, if not on the road to peace, at least was no longer on the highway to self-destruction.

20

THE COUNT OF MOUNTJOY WAS FEELING DEPRESSED AND neglected. These were emotions quite foreign to him, for he was a man of distinguished position and bearing, if not of distinguished ability, and accustomed to being the center of interest, of action, and of attention. His line, being of the noblest blood in Grand Fenwick next to the ruling family, had indeed supplied the diplomats and statesmen of the nation.

It was an ancestor of his, Count Robert of Mountjoy, who had negotiated the treaty of mutual assistance with England in 1402—a fact which he had been at pains to point out to the British minister during the latter's visit. To this, the British envoy had made the peculiar reply that in contrast with much that had happened recently, the treaty was a case, perhaps the only one on record, of too much and too early.

Another ancestor of the count's, Derek of Mountjoy, had achieved immortality by informing Napoleon, on the eve of Waterloo, that any further military adventures on the part of the Emperor in Europe would bring the double-headed eagle banner of Grand Fenwick into the fray on the side of England. The shock to Bonaparte's morale on receipt of this letter—it had been delivered by a courier from Grand Fenwick—was credited in the duchy with having contributed to the Emperor's defeat in that engagement.

With all this and much more in mind, the count was conscious that through no fault of his own he was letting his ancestors down. In the past few months he had been in the very center of events which had shaken the whole world—events which would not only be recorded in glorious pages in the history of Grand Fenwick, but in equally glorious pages in the history of every nation of

the globe. And he sensed that when that history was
written, there would hardly be as much as a footnote—
at best a short paragraph, perhaps with his name mis-
spelled—recording his own part in these great affairs.
The trouble, he told himself, was that diplomacy had
been taken out of the hands of those who by their birth
and breeding were best suited for its intricacies, and
handed over to uncultured and blunt fellows like Benter
and that man Tully Bascomb. There were no niceties to
the game any more, no delicate balancing and weighing
of the situations, no exquisite pleasure in finding exactly
the right words with which to promise everything and
guarantee nothing, which were the very essence of diplomatic exchanges.

All that had happened was that that fellow Tully Bascomb had threatened to blow up the whole of Europe
unless an effective agreement was concluded to outlaw
weapons of mass destruction. The thing was done almost
before he, the Count of Mountjoy, could take a hand.
That it had been done, he had to concede, was good.
But that it had been done in such a boorish manner,
quite without any reference to the protocol of diplomatic exchanges, shocked him beyond expression.

To save face, to secure for himself an incontestible
place in history when the whole matter was written up,
he needed to execute one capital stroke that would show
his true genius as a statesman. And he now knew exactly what this was to be.

It assuaged his stricken ego, to some extent, that the
whole plan had come to him during an unofficial and
unpremeditated conversation with one of the captive
New York policemen, just before the latter had been released following the signing of the peace treaty with the
United States. General Snippett and the four policemen
were being led from the castle of Grand Fenwick to the
border to be handed over to the American consul who
awaited them there. The Count of Mountjoy accompanied the little procession, and on the way, one of the
policemen, exuberant perhaps at the thought of returning
to his native land, had said, "That Gloriana is some dish."

"Precisely what do you mean by that?" the Count of Mountjoy had inquired.

"A cute patoot," replied the policeman.

"I fail to follow," said Mountjoy.

"Look, dad," said the policeman, "it don't matter to you now on account of your age and you probably got a wife and kids. But that Gloriana's a knockout. A real honeybun. A Cadillac with sex appeal, if you get what I mean. And one of these days some lucky jerk is going to meet her and pitch her the woo, solid gold, see? And then your little duchess's new address will be maybe Fifth Avenue, New York, and maybe Beverly Hills, and maybe both."

At this point the party reached the frontier and the handing over of the prisoners was effected. The Count of Mountjoy was not quite sure he understood all that the policeman had said. But he believed he got the gist of it. And the gist of it was frightening enough. It was to the effect that a rich American was likely to court the duchess successfully, marry her, and, with that, the whole succession to the ducal chair would be imperiled and the future of the duchy as an independent state placed in hazard.

All for which they had striven would then be lost, and that very night, such was the impact of this new line of thinking upon the count, he had sought out both Dr. Kokintz and Mr. Benter and discussed the matter with them. A plan had been devised to avert the danger —a plan, he flattered himself, which had originated with him—and he was on his way to the duchess now to secure her agreement to it.

Well enough, he told himself as he went for his audience, for others to hold the center of the stage and receive the applause. But it is in the behind-the-scenes manipulation that the true genius of statecraft lies. And as he thought of this, and pictured himself as the man behind the scenes, manipulating matters of the greatest moment, he felt better and held his silvery head higher and fancied that if the spirit of Disraeli were anywhere near, it would certainly be smiling with approval. Disraeli was one of his heroes.

He found Gloriana eating pomegranates in her private
study in the castle. She had eaten a great number of a
large supply which the American Secretary of State had
had flown to her, for the husks were lying on a silver
dish on the table and there was quite a mound of them.

"Don't scold, Bobo," she said. "They'll spoil if I don't
eat them all in a day or two. Besides, it relaxes my
nerves. I've been upset lately with all the delegates from
all the countries coming here and having to meet them.
I like the man from Saudi Arabia best. He refused to
bow to me. He said it was against his religion for a man
to humble himself before a woman."

"Before such a woman as your Grace, the act of bowing, far from humbling, elevates a man," the Count of
Mountjoy replied.

"You're such a nice person to have around, Bobo,"
Gloriana said. "Sit down and talk to me."

He did so, and so far unbent as to accept half a pomegranate, picking the ruby beads out of it delicately with
finger and thumb. He did this for a minute or two, and
then putting the husk on the silver platter, and read-
justing his monocle said, "Your Grace, I have served
your father for twenty years and hope that it will be the
will of God that I serve you for twenty more."

"I hope so too," said Gloriana warily, for she knew
that when the Count of Mountjoy talked of his loyalty
there was some kind of scheme coming up.

"My family," continued the count, "has served the
rulers of Grand Fenwick ever since the duchy was
founded. You will recall, your Grace, that my ancestor
Mortimer Persimmon was squire to Sir Roger Fenwick.
And it was after the storming of the mountain on which
this castle stands, when he fought side by side with Sir
Roger, that he was created count, and in honor of the
day given the title of Mountjoy."

"Yes, I know that," said Gloriana.

"And so, it is my dearest wish that the family of
Mountjoy should continue to serve the descendants of
Sir Roger for all time to come. And yet, this may not
come to pass."

"What do you mean?" asked Gloriana in some dismay. "You're not thinking of going away?"

"No, your Grace. The failure would not lie in my family but in yours."

"In mine?" exclaimed Gloriana.

"Yes," said Mountjoy. "In yours. The matter is a delicate one, but as the oldest of your counselors, I beg leave to mention it. To come directly to the point, your Grace is unmarried and so has no family. The line of Fenwick is in danger of extinction."

Gloriana blushed. "I'm not ready to think of marriage," she said. "Besides, there's nobody I want to marry." This latter statement was not true, for Gloriana knew perfectly well whom she wanted to marry.

The Count of Mountjoy leaned back in his chair, placed the tips of his long white fingers together and looked with a mixture of paternal fondness and judicial wisdom at his ruler. "Your Grace," he said, "is surely not under the impression that personal affection or desire is a factor in the marriages of those into whose hands have been placed the destiny of a people. Matters of policy come before mere romance. The marriage of a ruler is a unique example of a sacrament which has, shall I say, a political instigation. I will not belittle its religious significance for a moment. Indeed, were such a marriage purely a civil ceremony, nothing more than the mere stamping of a license and the signing of a register, it would have no great standing among the people. But its greatest purpose is temporal rather than spiritual, and I might add that the two of them are not necessarily at odds with each other.

"When one such as yourself is wedded," he continued, "the primary purpose is the strengthening of the line of succession. And this must be done not only with an eye to the physical health of the mate selected, but with an eye too to forming such a political alliance as will add to the security of the nation."

"You sound," said Gloriana icily, "as if you were going to breed horses."

"Your Grace will forgive the blundering words of an

old servant who seeks merely to serve her, and his country," the Count of Mountjoy said, lowering his head humbly.

"Bobo," replied Gloriana, still not quite mollified, "when you make gestures like that you need an audience bigger than one. But go ahead and I will try to look at the matter impartially. I suppose what you are leading up to is that you've been thinking it all out very carefully, and you've decided who I shall marry."

"It is my duty to think of such matters as this," said the count. "I have not been solitary in my thinking, but have consulted others who also serve as your Grace's ministers."

"You mean Mr. Benter," said Gloriana.

"He, and also Dr. Kokintz."

"Dr. Kokintz? He doesn't know about anything but birds and bombs."

"Those, I will admit, are his specialties. But he is a man of keen observation. And all agree that the alliance which I am about to propose would be the best possible to ensure and strengthen the succession to the ducal chair of Grand Fenwick."

"I hope," said Gloriana warily, "that you are not going to suggest that I marry the American minister because I won't do it. I've been reading about the Americans in a women's magazine and they're all cruel to their wives."

"Cruel to their wives?" echoed the count.

"Precisely. They treat them as equals. They refuse to make any decisions without consulting them. They load them up with worries they should keep to themselves. And when there isn't enough money, they send them out to work instead of earning more by their own efforts. Some of them even make their wives work so they can go to college. They are not men at all. They are men-women. And their wives are women-men. If I am to marry, I want a husband who will be a man and let me be a woman. I'll be able to handle him better that way."

"We believe—Mr. Benter, Dr. Kokintz, and I—that the person selected will fill your qualification completely," Mountjoy said, somewhat smugly.

"And who is this person?"

"Tully Bascomb."

"Tully Bascomb?" repeated Gloriana, and felt a hot blush begin to creep over her face.

"Yes. There are a number of reasons of great importance why your Grace should seriously consider him as a husband, ignoring certain boorish characteristics of his nature which must offend those of aristocratic rearing."

"Tully Bascomb has no boorish characteristics of which I am aware," snapped Gloriana, quite angrily.

"It pleases me that you should say so," said the count, a little surprised at her tone of voice, "for that removes the one reservation to the match which I myself had. As to the reasons why he should become your consort, the first must already be apparent to you. That is his descent from Sir Roger Fenwick, the founder of our nation. I am prepared to admit that I was somewhat hasty in making the charge that Bascomb had designs upon the ducal seat of Grand Fenwick. Nonetheless, the possibility remains that if he has no such designs now, these may appear at a later date. A young man who, contrary to instruction, wins a war against the United States is not to be trusted where ambition is concerned. United to your Grace in matrimony, such ambitions would be automatically gratified.

"The second reason for proposing this match is that Bascomb is very popular with the people of Grand Fenwick. He could, were an election held at the present time, secure an overwhelming majority of votes. You will recall that some time ago he confessed to your Grace that he was a politically confused man, in favor neither of democracy, Communism, or anarchy. If he were, at some later date, to stand for election, he would be returned to power heading some kind of political party which, not having been thought on before, would undoubtedly lead the nation to ruin. As coruler of Grand Fenwick, he would be removed from the sphere of politics and rendered harmless."

"I'm not at all sure that Tully Bascomb will ever be

rendered harmless," Gloriana said. "But continue, have you other reasons?"

"I have, but I have already been rebuked by your Grace with a reference to the breeding of horses, and do not feel at leave to proceed."

"Oh," said Gloriana. "Oh." And that was all she said for a while, for she had a great deal to think about.

Now that it was a matter of state that she should marry Tully, she found the prospect less pleasing than when it had been quite an impossible and unformulated dream on her part. She tried to think of being constantly in his company, and first she was thrilled by the prospect and then she was frightened. Perhaps he would take objection to some of her habits or mannerisms. Perhaps he would find her dull to talk to; a poor life companion for a man who had ranged the world at will. Perhaps he would criticize her because she could not cook a meal and he could make shoes and storm cities and fell trees and fashion arrows. Perhaps there was some girl in America, or Switzerland, or France, or one of the other countries he had visited with whom he was in love—or maybe even married to already.

Thinking of these things, Gloriana felt very lonely and scared and she looked at Count Mountjoy through eyes which were suddenly those of a very small girl and said, "Bobo. Do I really have to marry him?"

The count slowly nodded his head.

"But, Bobo. He may not want to marry me. He may not love me. He may be married to someone already. How am I to get him to ask?"

"It is not in his place to ask," Mountjoy replied gravely. "As ruler of Grand Fenwick, the proposal must come from you."

"From me? Oh no, I couldn't do that. I couldn't."

"You must. It is for your people and your country," the count replied. He rose solemnly, bowed and left Gloriana with a dish of pomegranates for which she now had no appetite at all.

21

THE DUCHESS GLORIANA GOT ON HER BICYCLE AND SAILED
down the mountainside from the castle along the road
which led to the Forest of Grand Fenwick and the cottage of Tully Bascomb. She had always enjoyed the ex-
citement of speeding down the mountain road to the
valley before, but now she wished she wasn't going so
fast. She wished she could hold the bicycle down to the
pace of a snail, and she tried to do so. But the brakes
weren't very good and the road was steep and however
hard she tried, the bicycle still picked up speed. Then
she thought maybe she would hit a stone or a rut and be
thrown and have to go to bed for a few weeks. But
there were no stones and no ruts and the bicycle continued inexorably on its way.

There were a lot of things worrying the duchess, but
foremost among them was how to propose. She had
tried a hundred combinations of phrases since her interview with the Count of Mountjoy a week ago, ranging
from "We command you as a loyal subject to marry us,"
to a humble "Will you please marry me?" But they all
made her sound like a hussy. So she had given up trying.
Then she was worried about how she should wear her
hair so as to make the proper impression. Should she let
it fall loose around her shoulders as she normally did, or
should she put it in a roll at the back of her neck, or
should she pile it high on the top of her head? There
was a great variety of hair styles in the magazines but
none designed specifically for such an occasion as this.
She wondered whether men had the same troubles, worrying about how they should comb their hair before calling on their girl friends to propose to them.

Another thing was her face. Normally she didn't wear
make-up. But she supposed that she really ought to on

this particular day. She had put some on, and there was too much. Then she had tried to take it off and it looked worse. She'd got the face rouge and lipstick off, but the eye shadow wouldn't come off. Instead it spread around her eyelids and made her look as though she had not slept for nights. Which was not far from the truth.

Clothes were another worry—a cotton print, a tweed suit, or an afternoon frock? Again there was no source of advice so she had settled on a tweed skirt and turtle-neck sweater. It was hot, but at least it went with the bicycle. But she was deeply aware as the road slipped by and the cottage drew nearer that she was as hope-lessly unready for the occasion as she had been when the Count of Mountjoy first confronted her with the ne-cessity for marrying Tully Bascomb. And when she final-ly got to the cottage, she was so nervous she could hardly get off the bicycle and knock at the door. Her heart beat so wildly before the door was opened that it was quite difficult for her to breathe. But some of her panic went when the door was opened not by Tully but by Pierce Bascomb, his father.

"Come in, your Grace," he said in his deep gentle voice. "We have hardly had a glimpse of you since the Tiny Twenty conference. Have they been keeping you very busy at the castle?"

"A little," said Gloriana.

"Well, don't let them put too much on you," Pierce advised. "Rulers must learn to let others do the ruling. That is the only way they can get out among their sub-jects, which is one of the most important aspects of government. Sit down while I pour you a glass of Pinot."

He brought a bottle and two wineglasses and poured a little wine into each glass. There was an awkward silence. Gloriana contemplated the stem of her wine-glass and Pierce looked at her with the same straight inquiring look which his son had inherited.

"You've got something on your mind," he said at length, "and if that is the reason you came here, why not tell me about it and get it over with?"

"Well," said Gloriana, "I was expecting to see Tully."

"Tully? He's in the forest, but will be back in about twenty minutes."

"I have something to say to him."

"Would you like me to leave when he comes?"

"I don't think so. It really concerns you too, I suppose."

"Oh."

There was another silence.

"Mr. Bascomb," said Gloriana suddenly. "How did my father propose to my mother?"

"Well," said Pierce surprised, "I wasn't there, but that doesn't make much difference because plenty of other people were. It was at the annual archery contest, and your mother, who came, as you know, from the southern end of the duchy, was a competitor. She did so well that in the mixed finals she was matched against your father. Your father knew your mother by sight, as everybody is known in Grand Fenwick, though they had not been formally introduced until the day of the contest. Your father was to shoot first for the grand prize, and his arrow pierced the butt in the dead center of the bull's-eye. Your mother's arrow, however, was so well aimed that it split his, and according to the rules of the contest, she was awarded the prize of the silver bow. When it was presented to her, he came down from his chair, picked her up and holding her aloft before all the people, cried out, 'Gloriana has won one prize, but I claim two. I vow before you all that I shall marry her.' That was the way it was."

"But I couldn't possibly lift Tully," Gloriana said, half to herself. If Pierce heard, he made no comment, but there was the suggestion of a twinkle in his eyes.

"Mr. Bascomb, please don't think me rude, but how did you propose to Mrs. Bascomb?"

"To tell you the truth," Pierce replied with a smile, "I never did. She proposed to me."

"How did she do it?" Gloriana asked eagerly.

"I'm not quite sure of the details. I was busy writing my first book at the time. I loved her, of course, but I didn't realize that I loved her. I had got to a chapter on robins and was having some difficulty because I was not sure of the incubation period of the eggs. I have always found with writing that when I get to a difficult part, it is better to just walk away for a while and the difficulty will resolve itself. I decided to call on Elizabeth's father, and went over to his house. We talked about a few trifling things and then he said, 'By the way, Pierce, I have been asked by my daughter whether I would consent to become your father-in-law. I welcome the proposal myself provided it coincides with your desires.' I did not quite grasp what he was saying and the poor man had to repeat the phrase two or three times before I caught his meaning. Then, of course, I was delighted— so delighted indeed that I kissed him, as I recall it, and shook his daughter's hand."

He laughed so heartily that he had to wipe his eyes and while he was still laughing Tully came in. He hesitated, stooping in the doorway which he filled with his bulk, on seeing Gloriana.

"Come in, son," said Pierce. "Gloriana has called to see you."

"Oh," said Tully. He entered and went over to the fireplace, where he stood with an arm upon the mantelpiece.

Gloriana had a feeling of panic. She did not know what to say, how to begin, what conversational route to follow to lead up to the important object of her visit. She wanted to fly from the room, and was almost on the verge of doing so when Tully said gently, "If there is any way I can be of service, your Grace, I am yours to command."

"I have an important matter to discuss with you," Gloriana whispered, feeling completely wretched. "It's a matter of state. But it's something personal too. It's more personal really than it is a matter of state."

"Whatever it may be," said Tully, "I will do all in my power to help."

"It's not really a matter of helping. It's a matter of co-operating—of working with me."

"Working with you?"

"Yes. Well, not exactly that." She looked appealingly at the older Bascomb.

"You say it," she pleaded. "You say it, like they said it for you."

Pierce looked from her to his son. "Gloriana wants me to become her father-in-law—that's it, isn't it?"

"Yes," Gloriana whispered.

"Her what?" asked Tully.

"Her father-in-law."

"Father-in-law! But you're my father."

"Precisely, and you are my only son."

Tully looked for a second from one to the other and then walked over to Gloriana and, taking her two hands, raised her to her feet.

"My father accepts proudly," he said, "his son humbly."

22

THE WEDDING WAS THE GREATEST SOCIAL EVENT OF THE year. It was international in scope, for not only the representatives of the Tiny Twenty, but also those of the Big Three were there to attend the ceremony. The President of the United States, breaking all precedents, announced that he would attend in person, and hardly had the news been given out than the Premier of the Union of Soviet Socialist Republics stated that nothing would prevent him also from seeing the pair united.

This announcement was received with rejoicing in all the Western nations, for it was interpreted as a promise of greater tolerance towards religious worship in Russia. The Prime Minister of Great Britain informed a cheering House of Commons on the following day that Her Majesty the Queen had expressed her intention also of being present at the ceremony, and taking their cue from this, the Tiny Twenty one by one decided to send not merely ambassadors but the heads of their nations to Grand Fenwick for the marriage of the Duchess Gloriana to her chosen consort, Tully Bascomb.

Indeed, so many people of such exalted position all accepted invitations to the wedding that Tully was gravely concerned about holding it in the castle, deep in whose bowels still lay the malignant and terrible Q-bomb.

"If anything were to happen to the bomb," Tully said, "hardly a country in the world would be left with a leader."

"That is the strongest guarantee there is that nothing will happen to the bomb," Gloriana said serenely.

There were many difficulties of a diplomatic nature attached to the limiting of the wedding guests. As a security measure, it was ruled that only the heads of the different countries, without any attendants, would be allowed into the duchy. But the President of the United States, it was discovered, was accompanied wherever he went by secret service men, and these could on no account be left at the border. An agreement was reached whereby the Presidential guard was permitted to accompany the President, but were dressed in chain mail to make them less outstanding among the forces of Grand Fenwick who filled the church. Apart from the fact that they carried pistols in their scabbards instead of the traditional broadsword, they were not too noticeable.

The Premier of the Soviet Union was also accustomed to being accompanied by a bodyguard, and these too were compelled to don mail. The Queen of Great Britain arrived with her bodyguard already in chain mail—scoring something of a triumph from the point of view both of diplomacy and etiquette.

The wedding was to take place in a small chapel which gave off the great hall of the castle. There was room in the chapel only for the principals at the ceremony. The rest had to remain in the great hall, where they could catch a glimpse of what was going on, for the chapel was at the top of a flight of six stone steps. The ceremony was held in the evening, timed to start just as the sun commenced to slip behind the rim of mountains which formed the western wall of Grand Fenwick. Gloriana and Tully were both dressed in the garments of the fourteenth century in keeping with the traditions of the duchy. The duchess wore a miter-shaped hat, from which a gossamer veil of finest lace draped loosely over her back to fall upon the ground as a train. Her outer gown was of azure, being in the form of a cloak pinned across her breast by a massy chain of gold. Below, her kirtle, which came to her ankles, was of ivory satin into which had been worked the Fenwick double-eagle crest in silver thread. Tully, towering over her, wore the loose bonnet drooped to one side, the embroidered jacket and cloak with fanciful jagged edges, the trunk hose and pointed shoes of the days of Chaucer.

In the matter of fashion, Dr. Kokintz was perhaps the most strangely garbed. He had been selected as best man, and had agreed to wear the striped trousers and cutaway coat becoming the occasion. But he would not be parted from the sports jacket of his own design, without the lapels, but with the multitude of pockets. So he had this under his formal cutaway instead of a waistcoat, and it could be plainly seen, though he had been parted from the batteries of pencil stubs and pens which he normally carried in it.

There was no instrumental music of any kind. Instead, when the bride entered the great hall of the castle to walk, on the arm of the Count of Mountjoy, up an aisle formed in the center, a chorus of men, in a gallery at the rear, commenced singing an ancient hymn in Latin, to be answered by a chorus of boys, the deep notes of the one splendidly contrasted with the high piping of the other.

Gloriana walked slowly, two pretty pages, their hair appropriately bobbed, and themselves clad in white satin, carrying her train. Behind came six ladies in waiting, in costumes similar to the bride's, though all of yellow. And when the duchess reached the altar rail, so nicely timed was the procession, it was to stand in a shaft of gold from the setting sun which flooded through a lancet window above. She was joined at the altar by Tully, and as the two knelt on faldstools together, the voices ceased and all in the great hall and the chapel at the end of it was silent. Some said that was the most touching moment of the ceremony; others that it was Gloriana's gentle but firm promise to love and cherish her husband, and his parallel pledge which contained the word "obey," making a nice distinction between ruler and consort.

When it was done and the benediction given, a great shout went up from all sides, and the Count of Mountjoy, the first to kiss the bride's hand, felt that this was truly his moment of triumph—that he had brought this union about.

Before the duchess and her consort went away for a

honeymoon, which was to include visits to all the capitals of the Western world, Dr. Kokintz had a private word with Gloriana and secured from her permission to enter the dungeon where the Q-bomb was kept. But no one else was to be allowed to enter with him.

And the bride and bridegroom had hardly set out for Paris in a plane provided by the French government, which had now been reformed following the settling of the matter of taxi drivers' overtime, when Dr. Kokintz addressed himself solemnly to his canary.

"Dickey," he said, "this little country is the natural product of one of nature's greatest upheavals." The canary chirped with what Dr. Kokintz took to be bright intelligence.

"Yes, Dickey," he continued, "these mountains around which form the walls of Grand Fenwick were caused by the thrusting up of the earth's crust during the cooling period, billions of years ago. And what happened once, may happen again. Do you know what would be the result if there were an earthquake here, or some pressure below the earth or on the other side of the world were to cause a major fault to appear in these mountains? I will tell you what would happen. The Q-bomb would explode. And all our efforts to secure the world from destruction would be canceled out."

He left the canary then and went down the spiral staircase that led deep into the rock below the castle to the dungeon where the Q-bomb was kept. The guards had received instructions from Gloriana to admit him to the dungeon, but no one else, and so stepped aside and opened the great door which creaked and groaned as it was thrust back. On a solid slab of stone in the center of the gloomy cell, cushioned on a pile of straw, lay the lead box which contained the bomb. Dr. Kokintz waited until the door had closed behind him and then walked slowly over to it. A lantern which he had brought with him threw a pool of light around his feet. He stopped and put the lantern down. Then he wiped his glasses, his hands trembling a little, and reached out for the bomb. Perhaps it was because he had forgotten the weight of it, perhaps it was because the light of the lantern was so poor that he misjudged the distance. Perhaps it was just nervousness on his part. Whatever the reason, the bomb slipped from his hands, trembled for a minute on the bed of straw, and then, as he watched it, paralyzed with horror, fell with a thump to the stone floor of the dungeon.

Nothing happened.

Dr. Kokintz, his face frozen with surprise, looked at it for some seconds. Then he picked it up, still cautious. He took a clasp knife from his pocket, and after working for a while, took one panel off the side of the bomb and peered inside.

"So," he said musingly, "a dud. That hairpin of Mrs. Reiner's, my landlady, which I used for a spring was of poor quality, and so we are all safe. It is a pity that neither she nor anyone else will ever know about it." He put the panel back, picked up his lantern, and left the dungeon.

As he passed the guards at the door one of them asked, "Is the bomb still in good condition, Doctor?"

"In excellent condition," Dr. Kokintz assured him. "It is a better bomb than ever."